He'd taken off his tunic, peeled down to his bare skin.

His chest was magnificent—broad and lean and olive tan. His abs were a rippling six-pack, all angled shadows, bisected by a light V of black hair.

He walked over to the basin, sat down on the rim and pulled off his riding boots. "What are you waiting for, *kalila*?"

She blinked. *Oh, lord.*

"You want to…" She glanced at the swirling water as he poured a handful of crystals into it and they began to foam. "Together?"

His brow rose. "That's generally how it's done. Unless you Americans have invented a new way I'm unfamiliar with?"

He obviously wasn't talking about bathing.

He untied the waistband of his trousers. They, too, dropped to the floor.

Leaving him completely, wonderfully, rampantly naked.

Not what she'd expected.

But oh. My. God.

Impossible to refuse.

Books by Nina Bruhns

Harlequin Nocturne

Night Mischief #25
**Lord of the Desert* #93
**Shadow of the Sheikh* #100

*Dark Enchantments
**Immortal Sheikhs

NINA BRUHNS

credits her gypsy great-grandfather for her love of adventure. She has lived and traveled all over the world, including a six-year stint in Sweden. She has two graduate degrees in archaeology (with a specialty in Egyptology) and has been on scientific expeditions from California to Spain to Egypt and the Sudan. She speaks four languages and writes a mean hieroglyphics!

But Nina's first love has always been writing. For her, writing is the ultimate adventure! Her many experiences give her stories a colorful dimension and allow her to create settings and characters that are out of the ordinary. She has garnered numerous awards for her novels, including a prestigious National Reader's Choice Award, three Daphne du Maurier Awards of Excellence for Overall Best Mystery-Suspense of the year, five Dorothy Parker Awards and two RITA® Award nominations, among many others.

A native of Canada, Nina grew up in California and currently resides in Charleston, South Carolina.

She loves to hear from readers, and can be reached at P.O. Box 2216, Summerville, SC 29484-2216, or by email via her website at www.NinaBruhns.com or via Harlequin Books www.eHarlequin.com.

SHADOW OF THE SHEIKH

NINA BRUHNS

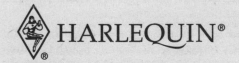

HARLEQUIN®

TORONTO • NEW YORK • LONDON
AMSTERDAM • PARIS • SYDNEY • HAMBURG
STOCKHOLM • ATHENS • TOKYO • MILAN • MADRID
PRAGUE • WARSAW • BUDAPEST • AUCKLAND

Recycling programs
for this product may
not exist in your area.

ISBN-13: 978-0-373-61847-7

SHADOW OF THE SHEIKH

Printed in U.S.A.

Dear Reader,

The Sheik. Since the breathtaking story penned in 1921 by E. M. Hull, the fantasy of being carried off by a handsome desert sheikh has captured the imagination of every woman who ever read that sizzling tale of passion, or has seen the groundbreaking movie based upon it. Who could forget Rudolph Valentino's sultry performance as the notorious hero who took what he wanted and won the heart of his reluctant heroine?

Shadow of the Sheikh is my modern retelling of the classic fantasy…with a slight twist. The hero, Sheikh Shahin, is an immortal shape-shifter. Which makes him even more dangerous…and attractive…to the heroine, Gemma.

Shadow of the Sheikh is book 2 of Immortal Sheikhs, a trilogy that features three American sisters living in Egypt for the summer who suddenly find themselves in the middle of a five-thousand-year-old war—and falling in love with three powerful men who are determined to possess them…forever.

Writing this series for Harlequin Nocturne has been amazing. As an Egyptologist, I have always wanted to set a book there. Now, finally, my dream has come true! And what a series. Based on the mythical conflict between the gods Seth and Horus, the story spins out a present-day continuation of the epic battle between light and darkness. You may be surprised how it turns out….

I hope you enjoy the continuation of Gillian, Gemma and Josslyn's frightening, sensual and most of all very romantic journeys to the twilight of the ancient gods as much as it thrilled me to write them!

Good reading!

Nina

For Eva Zamel,
who shared my youthful Egyptian adventures
and the joys of deciphering the secrets and
mysteries of that amazing country, both along
the Nile and at the Gustavianum.
xntš ib.k
Love you always

Once experienced, the desert life burrows into the blood and reposes there, never quite letting go the soul.

—Sir Richard Burton

Before the time of the pharaohs, each of Egypt's great gods and goddesses chose one mortal, a man, to serve as their high priest on earth. These men became demigods, and were granted great magical powers, including the ability to shape-shift. Each high priest in turn chose two-hundred loyal followers, the shemsu, to guard the god's temple and keep the scared rituals alive.

But Sekhmet, the lion-headed Goddess of War, Mistress of Dread and Keeper of a Woman's Moon, became discontent with the arrogant male demigods, and schemed to gift her temple priestesses with even more power. Sekhmet gave these women the secret of immortality.

The high priests were enraged, and demanded eternal life, as well. Sekhmet agreed. But...

She was a clever and merciless goddess, and demanded a price of the demigods. Over the course of a year she slowly drained the vitality of their blood. If not replenished, the high priest would die. So to preserve his immortality and regain his strength, each year the high priest must undergo a Ritual of Transformation...and drink the blood of a mortal woman.

He must become...a vampire.

Chapter 1

Present Day
The Nubian Desert, Upper Egypt

The sound of thundering hoofbeats came just split seconds before a half-dozen Bedouin riders burst around the far corner of the temple ruins.

Gemma Haliday leaped to her feet in alarm, the papers in her lap scattering around her like snow in the desert. She'd been sitting on a blanket in a sliver of shade next to the crumbling Temple of Sekhmet, quietly working on her current transcription, this one of a local vampire legend.

The camels bore down on her, hell-bent with

tassels flying, riders urging them on in loud shouts.

"Joss!" Gemma screamed to her older sister, who was sketching hieroglyphic inscriptions on the other side of the temple wall.

"Already here," Josslyn said right behind her, accompanied by the welcome sound of a shotgun being locked and loaded.

The beasts coming at them were huge, yet stopped on a dime at their masters' command, forming a snorting, braying semicircle around the two sisters. She and Joss were trapped, a tumble of massive stone blocks cutting off any possibility of retreat.

The riders were dressed in the traditional garb of nomad warriors—black trousers, black boots, billowing black *bisht* cloaks over tunics crisscrossed by leather weapons belts and straps, curved scimitars at their sides, flowing black turbans covering their heads and faces. The kind of outfits you hardly ever saw anymore, other than in pictures in museums.

The men themselves were huge, too. And they looked mean. Unsmiling. Like they meant business. Especially the guy in the middle. He sat tall in the saddle, his shoulders broad, his features arrogant. And he was staring right at Gemma.

Her pulse went into hyperspace. Her usually loose tongue forgot how to move. Along with her feet.

Stories of kidnapped women and ruthless slave traders ripped through her mind.

Oh. My. God.

Joss stepped forward so they stood shoulder to shoulder, the shotgun pointed at the ground but visible and at the ready. Josslyn was the oldest sister and always took charge in a crisis. Thank God. Gemma was more of a negotiator. Somehow she didn't think that was an option here.

"What do you want?" Joss asked the middle rider who seemed to be in command, using her firmest we-may-be-women-but-we-won't-take-any-of-your-male-chauvanist-bullshit voice.

The man didn't answer. Nor did his sharp black eyes stray from Gemma. They swept down her body, then back up, to drill her with a deep, penetrating stare.

She felt herself blush under the power of it. The look was blatant, unapologetic...and sexual. Like he was stripping her naked and laying her bare by the sheer force of his regard.

Unbidden and unwanted, a zing of response clenched low in her belly and tightened her nipples. The man was terrifying...but, she had to admit, sexy as hell. The kind of savage, untamed man who came to a woman in her deepest, darkest erotic fantasies. *Ho*-boy.

At some silent signal, the man's camel dropped

to its knees and he swooped down from it, landing on his feet in a flurry of dust and billowing cloak.

Joss raised her shotgun. "What do you want?" she repeated, louder, switching to Arabic.

Gemma's heart pounded like crazy.

Wordlessly, the man advanced on Gemma as though he didn't even see the weapon, which was impossible to miss because Joss put it to her shoulder and took aim right between his black eyes.

The good news was that the other riders didn't move an inch. The bad news was that Gemma couldn't either. She stood rooted to the spot, her feet like lead weights, her heart beating in her throat like a bird caught in a net. And still the man advanced on her.

"Stop. *Now.* Or I'll shoot," Josslyn ordered him sharply. She aimed the gun over his men's heads and started to pull the trigger. Without missing a step, the leader raised a hand and flicked the air as though brushing aside an insect. The gun made a clicking noise. Joss cursed.

With the same hand, he then reached under his robes and withdrew something. Gemma gasped, expecting a weapon—a pistol or a knife, or even a hypodermic needle.

It was an envelope.

She blinked in surprise.

He stopped in front of her. There was nowhere

to run. He was tall. Muscular. Hard. Too big. Too powerful. *Too* close. He was so close that when his eyes captured hers, she could see there was a ring of gold between the black of his pupils and equally black irises. *Predator eyes.*

She could smell his body—musky with the heat and the dust of the Egyptian desert, and spicy from some exotic oil of the kind men usually wore to please a woman. Before she could stop herself, her nostrils flared and she drew in a lungful of his arousing scent. His gaze snapped down to her nose. Then lower, to her lips as they quivered slightly.

Something brushed over her skin, hot and electric. Like an invisible wave of energy emanating from his powerful body. Or from that piercing gaze. The earth trembled under her feet, subtly, like a small temblor. Or maybe it was just her knees shaking.

She swallowed. Transfixed.

He reached out, grasped her hand and placed the envelope in it. "A note, from your sister," he murmured in perfect English.

She grasped the stiff square of parchment, the shock of his words rendering her even more speechless.

From Gillian?

With one last, bone-shivering sweep of his eyes over her body, the man turned on a boot, strode back to his camel and swooped up onto it. In less time than it took to realize he was leaving, the animal had risen again, and the riders had thundered away, leaving nothing but a storm of dust in their wake.

When the cloud lifted, they had vanished completely.

Stunned, she and Josslyn stared for a long moment at the empty space where they'd disappeared.

"What the *hell* was that?" Joss asked, eyes wide.

Gemma shook her head slowly. "Wow. He was…"

"Really pushing his luck," Joss muttered, lifting her shotgun to examine it. "I can't believe it misfired…" She broke it open and checked the cartridges, frowned, snapped it shut and fired off a round harmlessly into a nearby hillock. The blast echoed off the *gebel* behind the temple.

Gemma jumped. "Would you put that thing away! They might think we're shooting at them!"

Joss glanced up at the cliffs where they'd disappeared. "Somehow I don't think they're too worried about us."

Gemma followed her gaze and shivered, half-terrified the man and his mysterious riders would return.

Half wishing he would…

"Who do you think they were?" Josslyn asked thoughtfully. "Didn't seem like locals. Not even the usual nomad types. Have you ever run into anyone who looked like them on your ethnographic interviews?"

Gemma was a cultural anthropologist, an ethnographer, assistant professor at Duke University specializing in the bounty of traditional stories, myth and lore found here in this remote area on the west bank of the Nile, a bit north of the first Egyptian cataract. Josslyn was an archaeologist with the Royal Ontario Museum in Canada. Her current project was studying the hieroglyphic inscriptions of the Sekhmet temple they were standing in front of.

"Not unless you count Sheikh Shahin and his death warriors," Gemma answered, her voice tightening inexplicably on the notorious name. The villages in this area were rife with legends of his deadly exploits. And his lethal charm...

"*Death* warriors?" Joss's eyes bugged out, then rolled in comprehension. "Ah, you mean the evil shape-shifters the village women tell their kids about, to keep them from wandering into the desert and getting eaten by jackals. Yeah, call me crazy, but I don't think that was them."

Gemma wasn't so sure. She didn't exactly believe all the stories and legends she listened to the local village women tell, faithfully transcribing them word for word for posterity. But she did believe there were things out here that one couldn't explain. Egypt was a land of mystery and contradiction, the ancient blending with the modern in a way that defied logic or reasonable interpretation. She didn't even try. She just kept her mind open about what she saw and heard, and knew she'd be forever fascinated by the country.

And by that man, too. Oh. My. God. She'd never seen such a toe-curling exemplar of drool-worthy masculinity in her life.

"Oh, please," Joss said, spotting the speculative look on her face. "*Please* tell me you don't think we just met this death sheikh guy. You know it's just a *story*, Gem. He doesn't actually exist."

"I know. But damn, there was something about him…. Something mysterious and very…attractive." She shot her a sinister grin.

"No. Very *dangerous*," Josslyn corrected firmly. "Don't even think about going there, little sister. Look at what happened to Gillian. One eyeful of a mysterious stranger and she takes off with him, without a word to anyone. God knows where she is or what she's doing."

Gemma shook off her crazy feelings and looked down at the envelope in her hand. "Oh, I have a pretty good idea what she's doing," she drawled, earning an amused eye-roll from Joss.

"Jealous?" Joss teased.

Gemma made a face at her sister. "Get real." Though honestly? A little part of her might envy Gillian. Love had always been illusory for Gemma. Everyone kept telling her she just hadn't met the right man. Whatever. "Anyway, maybe this note will tell us where she is. I sure hope so."

Their baby sister Gillian had disappeared over a week ago after phoning to tell them she'd met an incredible man and decided to stay with him for a while at his nearby estate. As yet they hadn't started to worry—she was an adult after all—but it was good to hear from her.

Albeit in the most bizarre method of communication imaginable.

Gemma tore open the envelope and read aloud.

My Dear Loving Sisters,

I hope this note finds you well and happy. OMG! I'm in love! He is a wonderful man who has already given me the stars and the moon. There is talk of a wedding soon. Be thrilled for me!

Incredible news—our beloved mother may still be alive. I am following every clue to find out the truth about her disappearance. Speaking of which, don't worry, I have not disappeared.

Am spending time with my new man and playing detective. I promise to be in touch soon.

Love and hugs, Jelly Bean

Gemma blinked. Frowned. And felt suddenly unsteady on her feet.

"What?" Josslyn grabbed the note from her and read it silently again. Her face was a portrait of incredulity. Gemma swayed toward the nearest sandstone temple block and abruptly sat down on it. Stars? Wedding?

And Isobelle Haliday was alive?

The three sisters had practically grown up in Egypt, traveling first with both their parents, then later with just their Egyptologist father as he threw himself into his work, pursuing his dark demons after their mother's abrupt disappearance twenty years ago. She had vanished not far from here, and after ten years missing had been declared dead. Her father had refused to accept it. He had returned obsessively to search for her, season after season, year after year, eventually abandoning their South Side Chicago home for good. Until one day he chose to walk away from his life, from his daughters, and disappeared into the burning desert to be forever close to the woman he'd loved too much to get past her loss.

"This is insane," Josslyn said. "Our mother is *not* alive. It's impossible."

Gemma agreed. It *was* impossible.

And yet...

"They never found her body," Gemma pointed out. "What if she *didn't* die? What if she was kidnapped, or has had amnesia all this time, or..."

"Or nothing." Josslyn took an angry pace away. "Dad searched for almost twenty years and didn't find a trace of her. You *know* I wish it were true, Gem, but it's not. This is just Gillian being Gillian, still trying to fix things so everything will go back to being perfect, like it was before Mom died. But some things can never be fixed."

"You're probably right," Gemma conceded. "Especially now, if what she says about this new man of hers is true. The stars and the moon? A *wedding?* Jeez, she must really be serious about this guy."

Josslyn made a noise of disbelief. "After only a week? Sounds to me like the guy is angling for an American passport." Joss was ever the skeptic of the family.

"Didn't she tell us on the phone that he was an expatriate British lord?"

Josslyn snorted again. "And if you believe *that* load of bull, I've got a couple of pyramids I could sell you, too." She handed Gemma back the note and shouldered the shotgun, glancing back at the *gebel*. "In any case, why don't we pack it in for the day. I could definitely use a drink after all this bizarreness."

"Yeah. Me, too," Gemma heartily agreed.

They gathered their things and climbed into the Land Rover, making their way back to the small villa they'd rented for the season, each lost in thought.

Later, after dinner, sitting on the verandah sipping a cocktail together, they watched dusk settle over the valley. The view was spectacular. It never failed to fill Gemma with peace and a feeling of home. In the near distance, the Nile River was a broad, winding ribbon of silver green, reflecting the oranges and pinks of the setting sun. A flock of birds, hundreds of them, dipped and soared across the sky, all turning as one, their white feathers flashing in the fading rays of the day's light, their calls echoing off the water. The smell of the river and the surrounding cultivation fields was earthy and fecund under the spicy scent of an exotic vine that blossomed profusely along an overhead trellis, and rustled gently in the evening breeze.

She caught one of the flowers in her fingers and brought it to her nose, taking a deep breath.

It reminded her of…

Of *him*. The mysterious man on the camel. The scent of him.

She closed her eyes, shivering at the memory of his face, his penetrating gaze. The terror and the attraction she'd felt for him.

Then she thought about Gillian's note and all the shocking news it had contained in its few short lines.

How had such a man gotten hold of it? Of all people, why had Gillian chosen *him* to deliver the note? Was he a friend of her sister's new boyfriend? If so, what kind of dangerous people was she hanging out with?

"Are you worried about Gillian?" Gemma asked her sister abruptly.

Joss thought about it for a moment. "No, not really. Are you?"

"No," she admitted. Puzzled.

A moment later she asked, "Don't you think that's strange?"

Josslyn turned her head to peer at her. "How so?"

"Both our parents vanished here in Egypt, and now Gillian has, too."

"But she didn't vanish. She phoned us," Joss pointed out reasonably. "And now she sent the note. It's been only a week. She's probably spent the whole time in bed with this new guy, and would not appreciate our charging to her rescue."

"We couldn't anyway," Gemma returned. "We

have no idea what her boyfriend's name is or where he lives. I think that should be worrying us, don't you?"

"What are you trying to say? You think she's in danger?"

"I'm not sure," Gemma said. "It just feels...well, like we should be more worried."

"So let me get this straight. You're worried about not being worried?"

Gemma pushed out a breath. "I guess that sounds nuts."

"You could say that," Joss said with a wry smile.

"Okay, I was just checking."

But the more Gemma sat there and thought about it, the more it started to feel...wrong. She couldn't explain it. She wasn't worried about Gillian. And yet, something at the edge of her mind told her she *should* be worried.

One thing Isobelle Haliday, their true child-of-the-sixties mother, had taught them—at least Gemma—was never to ignore any signs the universe was trying to send you.

"We should try to find Gillian," Gemma said. "Just to make sure."

Josslyn's drink halted halfway to her lips. "And how do you propose we do that?"

"The nomads," Gemma said. "That group of riders who delivered the message."

"Not the British lord? He might be easier."

She shook her head. "If she is in trouble, if this guy is bad news, we don't want to alert him by asking people where he lives. I can ask about the nomads because of my work. Those men today, they have to know where she is, too."

"Uh. Yeah. But we have no idea where *they* are either."

"I can find them," she said. "I have informants in every village on the west bank within a thirty-mile radius. Someone's bound to know who they are."

Joss just stared at her.

"You think I'm losing it."

"The thought did occur to me."

"Humor me, then."

"Gem, even if you find these men and manage to survive a second encounter with them—which I have grave doubts about, by the way—who's to say they'd tell you anything?"

"Why wouldn't they?"

"Earth to Gemma! Did you *see* those guys? They didn't strike me as the talkative type."

She sighed. "Yeah, you're probably right."

She left it at that and dropped the subject.

But at the end of the evening's contemplation, she decided she was going to try anyway. She just couldn't ignore the niggling voice in her head telling her to pursue this.

Or the excitement in other parts of her body at the thought of seeing the sexy, mysterious stranger one more time.

She smiled. Two birds with one stone. Perfect.

Chapter 2

Sheikh Shahin Aswadi strode along the main corridor of Khepesh Palace, dwelling place of the followers of Set-Sutekh, God of the Hot Winds and Chaos, Lord of the Night Sky and God of Darkness. He was heading for the private audience chamber of its high priest, his lord and leader, the vampire demigod Seth-Aziz. As always, the luxury and opulence of Khepesh Palace dazzled Shahin's eyes.

Ever-burning torch sconces illuminated gleaming marble floors, soaring silver-clad columns, and elaborate carved reliefs. Gorgeous painted murals depicting scenes of the ancient gods graced every

stone wall. Normally the sight was awe-inspiring.
But today the glitter of silver and precious jewels
just made him wish for a pair of sunglasses.

Still, compared to the blistering heat and blinding
summer sun of the scorching desert above, the
cool, torch-lit halls of the underground palace were
soothing to Shahin's aching head.

It was all the fault of that damn woman. The
mortal from yesterday. He could not seem to banish
her from his mind.

Which was absurd. She had been a minor incident,
a bit-part in the epic play that was unfolding all
around him at the moment. A means to an end,
nothing more. *Sekhmet's teeth*, she hadn't even
been the object of the exercise in delivering that
blasted note. That had been her sister, the blonde.
This woman's hair was long and auburn, curling
over her shoulders in a thick cascade of autumn fire.
Clearly not the one planned for capture.

And yet, here she was, stuck in Shahin's mind,
her beautiful hair shimmering like a dying fire, her
blue eyes burning with reluctant attraction for him,
driving out all thoughts other than how he might
possess her.

A dangerous state for a man in his position.

Shahin reached the portal of the high priest's
audience chamber, took a deep breath to quell his
inappropriate thoughts, knocked and strode in.

"There you are! Come in!" Seth said, turning from where he was pacing the room waiting for him.

Shahin sketched a courtly bow to the high priest. "My lord." He nodded as well to Seth's sister, the priestess Nephtys, who smiled at him from the sideboard where she was pouring three goblets of wine. "My lady."

"What news do you bring?" Seth asked. "Any word of our enemy?"

"Things are quiet above, for now, but there is some small movement along the border. I fear Haru-Re may be slowly gathering his forces, as he'd threatened."

Seth's face betrayed neither anger nor surprise. "So you think it's to be war."

The animosity between the only two remaining ancient cults, or *per netjer* as they were called, led by the only two remaining vampire demigods, Seth-Aziz and his perpetual enemy Haru-Re, had been going strong for five millennia. It was an ongoing battle, an extension of the original war for supremacy begun at the dawn of Egyptian civilization between Set-Sutekh and Re-Horakhti, the two rival gods whom the high priests served. The ancient gods were gone now, but ever in hope of their return, the fight was carried on by their immortal followers, the *shemsu*. Although immortal was a bit of a misnomer.

Under certain circumstances it was possible for all human immortals, even the demigods, to succumb to death permanently.

But for Shahin, the battle he fought was not one of religion. His interest was far more personal. There was just one thing he hoped to gain from this war with the vampire Haru-Re.

Revenge.

"I think the Englishman must have betrayed us," Shahin told his leader. "Why else would Haru-Re's warriors be gathering at our weakest frontier?"

"Lord Kilpatrick will not betray us," Seth-Aziz said evenly.

Nephtys handed each of the men a goblet of wine. Shahin exchanged a worried look with her as he took his. "I truly hope your faith in him is rewarded," he said. "But we must proceed on the assumption that it is not."

"Yes," Seth said, his jaw tightening slightly. "I suppose you're right."

"And what of your other errand?" Nephtys asked Shahin. "Did you see this Josslyn Haliday, Lady Gillian's sister?"

Shahin raised a brow at her use of the woman's title. Gillian Haliday and her lover, Rhys Kilpatrick, were traitors, deserters who'd betrayed the *per netjer*. A gifted seer, Nephtys had prophesied a union between Seth-Aziz and Gillian. But the woman had refused and chosen Rhys, Seth's master steward, and fled to the enemy rather than marry the demigod. Which was another reason Shahin must rid himself of his unwelcome obsession with the redhead. He had no desire to involve himself in any way with the sister of a traitor, unless it be to teach her a lesson in obedience.

He couldn't fathom why Seth was actually contemplating bringing Josslyn Haliday into Khepesh. Shahin understood revenge better than most, but this was an invitation to disaster, if you asked him.

"Yes, I saw Josslyn Haliday," he told the priestess. "She looks...remarkably like her sister Gillian." Not a high recommendation in his book, but Seth would be pleased.

Nephtys's wine goblet paused in midair. "Indeed?"

Seth asked, "How did she strike you otherwise? Suitable as my consort, do you think?"

"Depends on your definition. She tried to kill me," Shahin replied drily. "With a shotgun."

Seth's lips curved and his eyes lit in interest. "So, a bit more spirited than the Lady Gillian. That is good."

Shahin barely resisted a snort. "You want my advice? Watch your back. Your immortality does not protect against a sharp blade to the neck or the right kind of poison. The woman is trouble. Mark my words."

Seth drank down his wine and set the goblet on the table with a *clack*. "I appreciate your concern. But I plan to rule this sister with an iron hand from the start. My erotic powers should keep the woman content and submissive in her role as my consort."

Shahin had his doubts. He'd seen the look on the blonde's face as she wielded that shotgun. He didn't think *submissive* was in her vocabulary. And as for Seth's powers, she had to consent before he could use them on her. Good luck with *that*.

"In any case, you delivered the note?" Nephtys asked, looking oddly distracted.

"I did," Shahin confirmed and told them of the brief encounter. Minus his attraction to the redhead, of course.

"Good," Seth said. "That should keep them from making a fuss about Gillian's disappearance long enough for you to fetch Josslyn here to Khepesh. When do you plan to take her captive?"

Shahin knew Seth-Aziz had need of a blood sacrifice fairly quickly. He'd been cheated of his annual Ritual of Transformation the night Gillian and Kilpatrick fled to the enemy. That was a week ago. The vampire needed to feed soon, or he would begin to weaken.

"I have a rendezvous on the borderlands with a

couple of my spies tomorrow," Shahin said. "Will two days hence be soon enough? I can push the meeting to the next day if you need me to."

"Two days will be fine. I'm not fading quite yet," Seth assured him.

"The sooner the better, my brother," Nephtys said, and kissed him on the cheek with a concerned frown. "You'll need all your strength for the coming battle with our enemy if Shahin is right about Haru-Re's movements."

Seth smiled affectionately at her, then jetted out a breath. "We must also deal with the third sister."

"Gemma?" Shahin asked, his focus sharpening. "You plan to take her as well?"

Seth's mouth thinned. "I have no choice. Even though she is bespelled not to be concerned, leaving one sister free would eventually attract attention to the fact the others are gone. People would start asking questions, even if she doesn't. We cannot bespell the entire world."

A low hum started deep in Shahin's belly, recalling the lushness of the redhead's body and the hot glint of desire in her eyes as she'd looked at him.

"Let me have the other one," he said. The request was out of his mouth before he realized he'd spoken aloud. He regrouped. "I'll take care of her, so she causes no trouble for you or for Khepesh."

Seth regarded him with a mild look. "You wish to have her?"

No, Shahin did not wish to have the woman.

He wished to have the woman's body. A not-so-subtle difference. But no sense mincing words.

"Yes," he answered.

"Why?"

Shahin hesitated slightly. Lord Kilpatrick had been Seth's best friend before his defection, and it had been the Englishman's most fervent cause to stop the age-old tradition of taking sexual slaves. Seth had listened to him, and long since put a stop to the practice at Khepesh.

But Lord Kilpatrick was gone now, his opinions as worthless as smoke in the wind.

"I wish to use her," Shahin said forthrightly.

Nephtys's lips turned down and she darted a glance at her brother, whose brow rose slightly. Nephtys agreed with Kilpatrick. She had once been a slave herself, forced to endure the bidding of their ruthless enemy, Haru-Re.

Hell, Shahin also agreed. His own sister had suffered a terrible fate at the hands of that same enemy. It was one of the reasons Shahin was so bent on revenge.

The difference was, Shahin was man of honor, not a brute who would abuse a woman. He had never owned slaves, or even *shabti*—human servants—nor had he ever in his life forced a woman against her will, and he never would. But if he read Gemma Haliday correctly, permission would not be an issue. She plainly wanted him. Persuading her to come to him shouldn't be a problem.

"I could keep her at my camp," Shahin suggested, "until Josslyn accepts her position as your consort."

Seth paced consideringly. "Hmm, it would tie up that loose end quite nicely."

"You may rely on it, my lord," Shahin promised.

"Very well," Seth said, coming to his decision and turning. "You may have the sister to amuse yourself. But take care you treat her well. I am trusting in your honor."

"She shall have no complaint," Shahin assured him. "I only hope I can say the same for myself, when all is said and done."

Chapter 3

The priestess Nephtys had made a huge mistake. And she wasn't quite sure what to do about it.

Slowly she walked through the silver gate of Khepesh Temple into the first courtyard. A large, rectangular room with silver papyrus-shaped columns rimming the walls, this was the Festival Chamber where the high priest led the immortals of the palace in feasting and celebrating their god.

She glanced around, remembering the day so long ago when she had been initiated into the *per netjer* of the followers of Set-Sutekh, becoming an immortal. How happy she had been on that day! Finally, there had been somewhere she truly belonged. She still felt that way, all these years later. Her adopted brother Seth-Aziz was the high priest, and Khepesh was her home. She would gladly die for it…and for Seth.

She'd been a young woman back then, her heart still aching from the betrayal of the man she loved—a man who had traded her away without a second thought to her love, because at the time she'd been a lowly slave, unworthy of a high priest's serious attentions. A quick sip of her blood, a thorough fucking, then instantly forgotten. She'd been a sensual curiosity, no more, mainly due to her pale skin and exotic cloud of wavy red hair.

But no longer.

Joining the *per netjer* of Set-Sutekh, Haru-Re's arch-rival, had been her first step toward a revenge she'd been desperate to wreak. And now, after so many, many years, that revenge was finally in sight.

Except…

In her eagerness to help her adopted brother win the love of his life, she may have brought ruin down on all of them, and doomed Khepesh to annihilation.

Last week had been the annual Ritual of Transformation, part pomp and circumstance, part sexual bacchanalia, where Seth-Aziz must partake of fresh human blood. He had also planned to take

Gillian Haliday as his consort. Even though Gillian had fallen in love with another, Nephtys had insisted they go through with it. She'd had a vision of the future where Seth was in love with Gillian, and she with him. But at the ceremony, disaster had prevailed; Seth had been deprived of his sacrifice, and the lovers had fled.

Shahin had said the two blonde sisters resembled one another. Could it have been *Josslyn* Haliday in the vision, and not Gillian after all?

Nephtys wanted to cry in frustration. How could she have been so wrong?

Considering the events of last week, it seemed a strong possibility. But she would not go to Seth with a mere suspicion. This time she must be absolutely certain of her information. She would not risk her brother's heart and the future of Khepesh again on just a possibility.

Determined to find a way out of the mess she may have wrought, Nephtys walked through the first courtyard and into the next, the Courtyard of the Sacred Pool. Sparkling water poured over the edges of the pool with a soothing noise; floating water lilies with huge round-rimmed pads bearing bright pink flowers scented the air with a sweet pineapple and spice fragrance.

A place of meditation, it should be calming to her nerves.

It wasn't.

Because she knew what she must do. And it terrified her.

Unconsciously, she touched the place on her neck where twin bite marks had nearly faded away. But the powerful magic still lingered there on her skin. Marking her. Cursing her. Horrifying her.

Calling to her...

Even at the touch of her own fingers, a shock of erotic sensation coursed through her center, as though *he* had touched her there.

Demigods only needed to feed once a year, but that didn't prevent them from doing it more often. Back when she'd been slave to Haru-Re, they had often indulged in blood play, simply for the intense pleasure it gave both of them. Like the most powerful of drugs, a vampire's bite was addictive. An addiction five-thousand years had not diminished. Five-thousand years of waiting and yearning.

And then after all that time, last week he had come to her.

But it had just been a dream, she told herself for the hundredth desperate time since the harrowing dream-visit from her former lover on the night of the ceremony. *Not real.* It couldn't have been. Haru-Re would have had to penetrate the sanctity and infallible security of Khepesh Palace to have come to her in the flesh. Utterly impossible.

Just a dream, she argued with herself.

But how could a dream have bitten her on the neck leaving his bloody marks? And left a touch-spell that still had the power to make her quiver with otherworldly pleasure…?

What kind of treacherous magic had Haru-Re learned since they'd last met and shared each other's bodies, to be able to do such a thing in a dream? The thought frightened her as nothing else could.

She prayed for strength to do what she must.

She walked through the portal to the inner temple, the holy of holies. Her *shemats,* the two young acolytes who had been tending the offerings, smiled and inclined their heads respectfully, then slipped away to give her privacy.

The temple sanctuary looked especially beautiful tonight. The torch-lined walls were clad in glittering silver, the floor made of obsidian so black it was like treading upon the empty void of space. The arched ceiling was fashioned of dark blue lapis lazuli, the exact color of the night sky, spangled with inlaid diamonds that sparkled and winked in the same constellations as the trillion stars over the desert aboveground. It never failed to fill her with awe.

There were six gorgeous, pedestaled altars, lined up three on each side of Seth's intricately carved obsidian sarcophagus, which also served as the large central seventh altar. They were all still overflowing with fragrant offerings of flowers, fruits and wine leftover from the transformation ceremony—the ceremony her brother had missed, thanks to Nephtys's costly mistake.

It was time to rectify that error and try to learn the truth about which sister truly belonged with Seth-Aziz.

But to do that meant to risk having a vision of Haru-Re instead. After that first time, he had come to her twice more in dreams. Would he be able to reach out to her through her visions, as well?

Again she touched the spot on her neck. A trill of sexual awareness spilled through her and she moaned in despair. How would she ever resist the pull of his command? He seemed frighteningly determined to recapture her loyalty—and her body.

She raised her palms and prayed to Set-Sutekh, Lord of Storm Winds and Patron of Chaos, to lend her the strength of his powerful will to stay strong.

Then she rose and made her way to her suite of rooms in the *haram*, the living quarters of the temple, seeking out her private meditation chamber. That was where she kept her best scrying bowl, the Eye of Horus.

She lifted the bowl and set it down amidst a scatter of soft floor cushions, and with a wave of her hand she lit the hundred or so delicately scented candles that surrounded it.

She took a deep breath.

"Bring me a vision, oh Eye of Horus," she pleaded softly as she poured water from a sacred pitcher into its depths. "Please, please, let me know which of these troublesome sisters is meant to bring my brother happiness." As a prayer it lacked grace, but it was all she could manage in her present state of mind.

The sparkling clear water rippled gently in the bowl, spreading a feeling of peace through her limbs.

But when the vision came, stark and brilliant like a reflection of the sun's rays, it brought nothing but dismay and confusion. The woman Nephtys saw was not the blond sister from her previous vision. This woman had hair the color of flame. Even from the back, it was hair that made her gasp in recognition.

It was her own.

She was not here at Khepesh, but in the Palace of Petru, the stronghold of their enemy. And she was kneeling in submission before its master, Haru-Re.

Sweet goddess Isis! What had she done?

Chapter 4

Gemma Haliday was not normally an impetuous sort of person. And this was exactly why.

Shading her hand against the blazing midday sun, she watched the dust of that little urchin Mehmet's hastily retreating donkey rise in an ever-diminishing plume toward the sky. She should have known better than to hire the boy as her guide. Gillian had sworn he was honest—as far as it went for a native guide on the west bank of the Nile Valley—but had failed to vouch for his reliability.

Obviously it sucked.

What had she been *thinking* of, coming out here like this? Unfortunately, she knew exactly what she'd been thinking of. Or rather, *whom*. The mysterious man from yesterday had been with her all night long, starring in dreams that made her blush to remember.

So where was he now, this handsome desert sheikh of her dreams? She could use a little help here.

At least the black hawk that had been circling above her for the past several miles hadn't abandoned her. Yet.

Gemma sighed in resignation and turned her little mare, Bint, in a three-hundred-sixty-degree circle, taking her bearings. Well. Whatever bearings one could get out here in the middle of freaking nowhere. Literally. Nowhere.

There was no sign of the oasis that was her destination. Big shock.

Behind her was the slight craggy rise on the horizon marking the top of the *gebel*. The rugged cliffs were the distinct border of civilization—both ancient and modern—the universally recognized line in the sand beyond which anyone who valued their life dared not venture.

Anyone, that is, but Gemma.

Fool that she was, she'd believed Mehmet when he'd told her he knew of the black-clad nomads she was asking about, and was willing to lead her to their encampment at an unnamed oasis out in the western desert.

Not one of her more brilliant moments.

She was now well above those cliffs, up on a sand-covered high desert plateau which marched on in undulating sweeps for a thousand desolate miles to the west. Should she go on? Hope she was close enough to spot the telltale palms of the watering hole on her own? Or should she turn back...? It wasn't like she could get lost, really. Head east and you'd hit the Nile eventually. The real problem was the possibility of running out of daylight or drinking water. The burning sun overhead was brutal, easily fatal to those who weren't prepared. But the night was even worse; the nasty creatures that lived out here were largely nocturnal. Snakes. Scorpions. Hyenas. Jackals. And predators of the two-legged variety...

She let out a frustrated sigh. Oh, what the hell. Gillian was probably fine, Gemma told herself. *She* was the one who'd end up hyena bait if she didn't find her way back to the villa before sunset.

At a faint rustle of whispering sand, she shivered and peered around at the ground below Bint's hooves. A dark shadow flitted past. She tipped her gaze up to the sky and spotted the hawk, still flying lazy circles above her. For some reason the large bird of prey had royally spooked Mehmet. Enough so that five minutes after it started trailing them the boy had taken off like a frightened jackrabbit heading for home.

Gemma was very familiar with the stories the locals told about the mythical black hawk, *al Shahin*. That the bird was really one and the same as Sheikh Shahin, leader of the death warriors, an immortal shape-shifter who served Set-Sutekh, the ancient God of the Underworld. The mystical hawk was said to be a harbinger of death, that those who saw it should run for their lives. Which was just what Mehmet had done, the little brat.

The hawk above glided down closer to her, sweeping past in a rush of wings and whistling air, then soared up to ride the thermals just above her head. A shivering thrill went through her. She couldn't believe he'd come so near!

He was incredibly beautiful. His matt black feathers were sleek and long, his scalloped tail fanned and elegant. He was big, his wingspan wider than her outstretched arms. As she watched him, his head cocked and his piercing black eye focused on her, as though he were deliberately studying her, as thoroughly as she was him. Sizing her up.

That's when she noticed the gold band around his pupil. *Omigod!* Just like the man's yesterday!

Gemma's arms bloomed with goose bumps.

Could man and hawk be one and the same? *Sheikh Shahin,* the shape-shifter?

Wow.

Ho-*kaay.*

She was officially losing it here. Too much sun. And *way* too much imagination. Time to turn around. This had been a really bad idea anyway.

She reined the mare back toward the *gebel* and home. Suddenly, the hawk swooped down in front of her, letting out a blood-curdling avian cry. Gemma screamed as Bint reared, pawing the air, panicked by the predator's attack. Then the horse turned and bolted in the other direction, galloping deeper into the desert.

"Whoa!"

The hawk wheeled and flew up into the sky behind them.

Pulse pounding, Gemma reined in her mount, quieted her, and turned her around again. This was too weird. *Definitely* time to get out of here. She kicked Bint into a canter.

But the hawk came at them again, spooking the terrified horse back around to the west.

Gemma's pulse took off at a dead run along with Bint. Her hands started to shake as she struggled to get control of the panicked animal, her heartbeat thundering, her mind in a whirl of stark disbelief. She was nearly as frightened as her trembling mount.

What the hell was going on? And why, oh why, hadn't she thought to bring along Joss's shotgun?

After two more tries, both she and the trembling horse gave up and stopped turning for home.

It was like the hawk was toying with her. Steering her westward. Preventing her from following Mehmet back to the Nile Valley and the villa. Taking her…somewhere.

Which was just plain crazy.

Wasn't it?

By now both she and Bint were breathing hard and the poor horse's eyes were wild with fear. She decided to wait it out. It was still early afternoon. She had time and plenty of water. Eventually, the hawk would get bored with its game, and leave her alone. Meanwhile, she could search for the oasis.

So farther and farther into the western desert she rode, through the waves of shimmering heat that rose from the brown earth. Until the rocky ground gave way to golden dunes, and when she looked over her shoulder the crags of the *gebel* had disappeared completely below the horizon. Leaving her with no landmarks by which to steer home, other than the sun. And still no sign of the oasis. How far could it be? Mehmet had never said.

Gemma pulled out her water bottle and took a long drink, trying to calm her jangled nerves and to wet her throat, which had gone dry as the desert sand around her. She was really starting to worry.

Tipping her head up for a quick look, she realized with a start that her tormentor was gone. The black hawk had vanished. *Oh, thank God!* She quickly capped her bottle, wheeled her mount around and kicked Bint into a run.

And galloped straight into the path of a half-dozen men on camels moving swiftly toward her, the wind filling their cloaks like the wings of death.

Chapter 5

Through battle, treachery and magic, nearly all the vampire demigods who once flourished in Egypt have been destroyed. Today, only two still live to lead their shemsu—*Seth-Aziz and Haru-Re.*

It was déjà-vu.

The same bunch of black-clad warriors bore down on Gemma as the day before, but today, they looked twice as terrifying. Especially without Joss and her shotgun at her side. Gemma tamed her fear and pulled up, feeling mouse-small as the disdainful camels thundered up and completely surrounded her little mare. Again no escape.

Her heart nearly stalled in her chest, but she reminded herself that this was why she'd come. *She* had sought *them* out.

Him, a provoking little voice singsonged in her head.

Okay, fine. Completely irrational, she'd wanted to see *him* again. The man in her dreams. The man who had single-handedly compelled this fool's errand.

She scanned the circle of men, seeking their leader. And found him, his black eyes studying her with a sinister air of deliberation.

Her pulse spiked painfully. She swallowed down her rising apprehension, and said, "Thank God I found you!" ignoring the fact that *they* had in fact found *her.* "I'm afraid my guide deserted me. I was hoping to...to—"

To what? The sight of the object of her lust sitting up there on his camel, a man so powerful, so obviously unfettered by the bounds of civilization, even more gorgeous and arrogant than she remembered, sucked out every one of her brain cells. The real reason for her journey became tangled with heated memories of her erotic dreams. *Lord.* What *was* she hoping for, here? "Um..."

His black brows rose.

"—to ask you a few questions about my sister," she managed to recover her wits enough to say.

He continued to watch her, the expression on his handsome face hard, emotionless. Silent.

"Since you, um, delivered that note from her," she went on gamely, "you must know where she is. How she's doing…" Again her words trailed off. Did he even understand her? Yesterday he'd spoken English. Well, one sentence, anyway. "My sister," she said in Arabic.

"I know what you meant," he said, again in flawless English. He glanced at her mare. Then moved his camel forward. Before she knew what was happening, he swept her off her horse and onto his own mount, like she weighed nothing.

"Hey!" she squeaked, alarm rushing through her. "What do you think you're—"

"You will come with me," he said, pulling her in front of him on the saddle. One impossibly strong arm banded around her.

Just as in her dream.

Except this was all too real.

"Wait!" She struggled against his hold. It tightened.

He made a clicking sound and the camel lurched forward, accelerating into a run, followed in tight formation by the others. Her mare galloped along behind as though on a lead.

Panic surged through her. "Where are you taking

me?" she demanded, still fighting him as best she could.

"My camp."

The rocking gait of the camel pitched her back more firmly against his chest. His other arm came around her. A spill of energy, male and potent, sizzled through her at his touch.

"Is my sister there?" she asked, seeking desperately for a reason for the hijacking.

Other than the obvious.

Just as in her dream.

"No."

Somehow, she'd known that. She fought a tremble of terror…and a small tingle of unwilling excitement.

"This is kidnapping!" she cried, trying to pry herself from his grip.

He didn't comment. Just clicked again and the camels went faster.

"What do you want from me?" she demanded, but it came out sounding a lot more uncertain than she'd intended.

In answer, his hand splayed over her ribs, his thumb grazing the underside of her breast. Her nipples zinged to attention. Her body sang with dismay.

He put his lips to her ear and whispered roughly, "Everything."

Oh, God.

Somehow she'd known that, too.

She should be terrified. Hell, she *was* terrified. Had *been* terrified from the first moment she'd seen him coming for her—for there hadn't been any doubt that he'd come for her. Not to rescue her from being lost. Not to tell her where he'd gotten Gillian's note. But to take her. Capture her and bring her to his place of hiding.

To his bed.

She'd seen it written plainly in his eyes, even yesterday. Which was probably why she'd dreamed all night of his doing just that.

She was terrified, all right.

But more by her own reaction than by him, or by what was happening.

Because, to her horror, she realized she *wanted* this.

It was impetuous and reckless, and no doubt dangerous as hell.

But she wanted him, oh how she wanted him! And everything he planned to do to her…

He drew his *bisht* around her, the heavy native cloak protecting her from the wind and the dust. His scent, musky, masculine and already arousingly familiar, wrapped itself around her along with the thick cloth. By slow degrees, she relented and let her body lean back against his broad chest. She stopped fighting his hold. But she couldn't quite tame the trembling in her limbs.

This was so unlike her. Never in a million years would she have believed herself capable of feelings like this. She was the one who *listened* to the stories and tales of adventure that others had experienced. Always the audience, never the teller or the one who lived them. Her fantasies lived strictly on paper, or in her dreams. Never in real life.

But this was one fantasy she could not deny herself. It was as though the sensual smell of him held a powerful spell that worked its magic as she breathed it in. Tempting her. Arousing her. Seducing her to his will.

On and on they rode, the smooth lope of the camel lulling her to relax more and more. She closed her eyes and lost track of time, acutely aware of the hard male body pressed into hers, the strength of his arms as he held her close, and the aching thrum of desire that pulsed between her legs.

His hand slipped beneath the cloak and sought out her shirt, finding its row of buttons.

She'd dressed in practical clothes for the trek into the desert, khaki riding pants, knee-length boots, long-sleeved khaki shirt, a Blue Devils baseball cap which she'd lost during the struggle.

She held her breath as the man's fingers

maneuvered the top button open. And the next. And a third. And then his hand slid over her breast.

Her breath sucked in. Heat streaked through her flesh.

His fingers tugged down the lacy edges of her bra. "When we reach camp I will burn this," he said.

"Why?" she asked, momentarily stunned.

He cupped her breast. "I want you free of encumbrance and ready to my hand," he murmured against her hair. His thumb brushed over her nipple.

"Oh!" she gasped softly, a jolt of desire arcing through her. "Ohhh," she moaned on a quivering exhale as he gently pinched it.

And that's when she realized she was in even bigger trouble than she ever imagined. Because as his hand closed intimately around her breast and her body caught fire, she knew she had no will to resist this man. She would do anything he asked of her.

Anything at all.

Shahin had bespelled the woman. He had invaded her dreams. He had made her want him with a burning need matched only by his own. He had made her willing and pliable to his touch. To his possession.

The spell was working.

Gemma Haliday was putty in his hands.

And Shahin liked it. She was pretty. And soft. And filled his hands perfectly. He might just let the spell continue after they got to camp, instead of lifting it as he'd planned.

Kilpatrick had often said in his crusade against unwilling seduction that there was no challenge in making love to a woman who couldn't say no. Normally, Shahin agreed.

On the other hand, keeping the spell on Gemma intact would cut out a whole lot of unnecessary drama. He was short on time, and long on need. With Haru-Re on the warpath, Shahin had been so busy guarding the borders and running his spies that he'd hardly had a chance to sit down for decent meal, let alone find a woman to share his bed for a night or two.

Gemma would be a very welcome addition to camp life. For a while.

He had no intention of keeping her, of course. Not for the long-term. Even if he could imagine spending eternity with the same woman—which he couldn't—there was no place for a female in his world. He'd been down that road before—the biggest mistake of his life. It was the woman he'd once thought he loved who had sold his sister to Haru-Re, all for a promise of power and wealth. His parents had followed, and his father had died avenging her cruel fate. His mother was still a captive at Petru. Because of a faithless woman, Shahin had no family.

No, women were deceitful, untrustworthy creatures, and there was only one thing he wanted from them.

Gemma Haliday was no exception. He would enjoy her bounty, and after he grew tired of her, Seth-Aziz would rule on the woman's future: whether she would become a *shabti*—a human servant robbed of her will—or invited as a full-fledged initiate into the *per netjer* to become an immortal follower of Set-Sutekh. It was up to her to accept the coming revelations or not. She could join them willingly or unwillingly. But she *would* join, one way or another. Her sister's treason had seen to that.

Meanwhile, Shahin would have the use of her. Her lush curves under his hands felt good, reminding him of how long it had been since he'd enjoyed the delights of a woman's body.

He had no desire to delay his pleasure with this one. But he had been out on patrol along the borderlands with a small troop of the Khepesh guard, which he commanded, when he'd felt the nearness of her here in the desert. He hadn't expected her to come so soon. Normally, it took more than one night of dreams to influence a mortal's behavior to this extent.

He'd had the troop shift and detour to pick her up. Although it was an inconvenience having to stay in human form to transport her to camp, the pleasures that awaited him tonight far made up for it.

Meanwhile, he and his men needed to finish the patrol, which included checking on a remote outpost where two of his best spies werc based. They were approaching it now.

The camels slowed and he withdrew his hand. "Button your shirt," he ordered. "And when we get there, do not speak, even if addressed."

"When we get where?" She glanced over her shoulder at him, her eyes soft and heavy-lidded with arousal.

His need grew stronger and he barely resisted leaning over her for a kiss. But he wanted more than a quick tonguing. She would keep. And so would his need.

In answer, he tipped his chin at the rocky edge of a wadi just ahead. The dry wash, carved out by the waters of an ancient flood, provided the best cover for miles. And the only shade.

The woman knew Egypt well enough that she didn't question their destination.

"Why can't I speak?" she asked, doing up her buttons. Plainly, she didn't know *him* well enough.

"Because it is my wish."

"What if it's my wish to talk?"

Irritation flashed through him. "You will do as I say."

She glanced back at him again. This time her eyes were clear and cool. "And if I don't?"

"By the tail of Anubis, you will!"

He heard her puff out a breath and mutter something, but could only make out, "...*not* part of the fantasy..."

He drilled his fingers into her hair and turned her so she'd have to look into his eyes. "Did you not consider," he asked in a low growl, "that you are part of *my* fantasy?"

She blinked. Her tongue peeked out and swept over her lower lip. Again he had to restrain himself from taking that impudent mouth and teaching it to obey.

Later.

Letting her go, he exchanged a few quick words with his men as they crested the edge of the wadi and lined up the camels along it. From a short distance away came the yip-yipping of a jackal.

He glanced down at the woman sharing his saddle and hesitated. He should throw a spell of oblivion over her so he wouldn't have to deal with her as he heard his spies' reports. But the sooner she realized what she was involved with, the sooner she would accept her future. Or not.

"You may see things here you don't understand,"

he told her as they descended into the depths of the wadi. "Do not be afraid."

She turned and searched his face. "What kind of things?"

"These men are…a bit wild. The sight of a female may cause a stir."

"I see."

No, she didn't. But she would soon enough. "Stay behind my back at all times," he ordered her sternly. "I mean it, Gemma."

She looked startled. "You know my name," she accused. "How?"

He pinned her with a pitying look. "Of course I know your name. Do you really think your capture was random? That I didn't know exactly who I lured to meet me in the desert?"

Stricken, she stared at him, her expression reminiscent of an enemy just before Shahin's sword severed the bastard's neck.

"What are you talking about?" she asked hoarsely. "Who *are* you?"

He touched her cheek, running his fingers down to her jaw. "You've already guessed who I am, *kalila*—sweetheart. Earlier, when you looked into my eyes as I flew above you, I felt your recognition."

She frowned, then started to shake her head. Suddenly, her frame went rigid. "No," she whispered. Disbelief slashed across her face.

"Yes," he assured her. "My name is Shahin Gameel Aswadi. But most people know me simply as *Sheikh Shahin*."

Chapter 6

"That's r-ridiculous," Gemma stammered, clearly shaken. "*Sheikh Shahin* d-doesn't exist. He's just a legend."

Now was as good a time as any to disabuse her of her romantic fantasies. It would have been nice to let her keep them for the coming night, but Shahin had no patience for subtlety. She would find out the truth of the matter soon enough anyway.

"As you can see, I most assuredly do exist. Although I suppose my prowess might be considered legendary," he added drily.

Her voice choked with distrust, she surprised him by saying, "Prove it."

He brushed his thumb over her lower lip, deliberately dragging it down a fraction. Enough to convey his meaning. "Oh, I intend to."

A blush ripped across her cheeks and she turned away. "Not what I meant."

He just smiled, his body stirring with anticipation of the night ahead.

But they had come to the mouth of the hollowed-out wind cave where his spies made their base camp, so he urged his camel to the ground and dismounted along with his men. He reached up and swung Gemma from the saddle down to her feet. He removed his *bisht* cloak and draped it over her shoulders. Not to cover her. Unlike their modern counterparts, the ancient Egyptians—and the residents of Khepesh—treated their women as equals, and did not force any woman to hide her beauty beneath a veil and burka. But rather, Shahin covered her with his garment to mark her as his.

It looked good on her.

"Wear this and there will be no doubt to whom you belong," he said.

"I don't belong to anyone," she returned with a scowl, but nevertheless wrapped the cloak around her body.

An uncharacteristic barb of possessiveness caught in his chest. By Osiris, she *did* belong to him! He opened his mouth to tell her so, then quickly snapped it shut again. *Thot preserve him.*

Had he lost his mind? Only a witless fool would want to possess *any* woman for longer than the fleeting physical pleasure she could bring him. He'd gone down that road before and lived to bitterly regret it. He'd learned his lesson the first time a woman deceived and betrayed him. It would also be the last. And if he needed further evidence of the untrustworthiness of the creatures, he need look no further than his good friend Rhys Kilpatrick. He'd also fallen victim to a woman's trickery, had trusted her with his immortal life. See where that had gotten him—in the camp of the enemy, his home and friends lost to him, and a death sentence hanging over his head.

Gemma was that woman's sister. Shahin must never forget it.

Dismissing the whole distasteful feminine subject from his mind, he strode to where his men had gathered. They, at least, he could rely upon.

"Auwa!" Shahin called into the cave. "Time to wake up! Show yourself and greet your captain!"

The growl of a jackal answered him from the depths of the cave. Behind him, he heard Gemma gasp. Her body scooted closer to his back.

A few seconds later up on the wadi, a large

mountain lion padded to the edge and peered down at them. It snarled in greeting.

"Asad! Get down here." Shahin beckoned with a hand. "I am anxious for your report as well."

The lion padded easily down the steep incline. At the last few yards he crouched and leaped, his human form materializing in midair to land gracefully on his feet with a twist and a grin. Show-off.

From behind Shahin came a silence so thick you could slice it with a saber.

Auwa trotted out from the cave and also shifted to human form. With a smooth stretch onto his hind legs, the jackal unfolded into a compact, muscular man with beady eyes and a long nose which he jerked hungrily in Gemma's direction.

That's when she screamed.

Shahin spared a glance backward in annoyance and threw a calming spell over her. The scream choked off, but her eyes remained wild with fear and disbelief.

He signaled the men to sit for their meeting. Then with a hand to her shoulder, he urged her down behind him before she collapsed.

"Welcome to your new world, *kalila*," he murmured with just a hint of smile. "Now if you'll excuse me for a few minutes, I have some business to conduct before taking you home."

Please, God. This could not be happening.
Gemma struggled to slow the two-minute mile of

her heartbeat and quell the panic doing somersaults in her stomach. This was insane!

What she'd just witnessed was not possible. And yet, it had happened. In broad daylight. Right in front of her eyes. Two animals had turned into men, and they were now chatting away with the one who called himself Sheikh Shahin and claimed to be a hawk, as though there was nothing strange or unusual about any of it.

Shape-shifters!

Just like the countless stories the villagers had told her over and over in her ethnographical work. There'd been no doubt the locals believed their tales of the shape-shifting guardians of the old gods. But Gemma had never taken the tales as anything other than myth. Had always chalked up the villagers' staunch belief in them to rampant superstition and lack of education. What rational person wouldn't?

Just now when she'd dared Shahin to prove who he was, it had only been to flatly discredit his outrageous assertion. Not from any remote belief he was who he claimed.

But *could* it be true? Could it all really be true?

Unless she was hallucinating or going mad, it had to be. There was no other explanation for what she'd just seen.

Not that *that* made her feel any better. "Welcome to your new world," Shahin had told her. But that world was crazy, out-of-control. She wanted the old one back!

Or...did she? The ethnographer within her—who wanted to ask the shape-shifters a million questions—warred with the coward who just wanted to hide her head in the sand and pretend it was all just a hallucination. That she wasn't stuck in the middle of the desert with a man legend said could change into a hawk, along with his troop of death warriors, inhabitants of an otherworld she was just superstitious enough to credit as a dim possibility.

God help her, what should she do?

First on the list was not to think about that *other* thing he'd said earlier. Involving the word *capture*.

Because surely he didn't intend to *keep* her? It was one thing to spend the night with a dangerously attractive man, indulging in a scorching-hot, if majorly ill-advised, desert sheikh fantasy. But she wanted to go home in the morning. She *needed* to go home in the morning. The alternative was unthinkable.

She sat there now on the ground behind him, taking nervous peeks at the men sitting on their heels in a circle engaged in intent conversation. Were they all shape-shifters? Or just Shahin and the two she'd seen...change?

God. She couldn't even be*lieve* she was asking

herself that question. Joss would think she'd finally flipped over the edge.

Hell, maybe she had. Since her frightened scream, an unnatural calm had wrapped around her along with Shahin's cloak, making all of this seem completely unreal.

Or maybe she was still dreaming.

She pinched herself hopefully. Nope. No such luck.

Suddenly, the men all stood. The two shape-shifting spies eyed her warily. The others headed for the camels.

"Let's go," Shahin said and extended his hand to help her up.

Which was when, in that war in her head, the coward won out.

"Um, look…" she began, brushing the dirt from his *bisht* and handing it back to him. "I really don't think this is such a good idea, after all."

"What isn't?" he asked, slipping it on.

She started to walk toward her mare, which was standing amidst the much larger camels contentedly munching on the green leaves of a small bush. "Me going with you," she answered. "I should get back to the villa. Josslyn will worry, and—"

He caught her arm and changed her direction, firmly steering her toward his camel instead. "The sun will be going down soon," he said. "I couldn't possibly let you ride across the desert alone at this hour. Besides, you'd never find your way. We are a long way from Naqada."

The fact that he was probably right on all counts did not reassure her all that much. But he didn't seem to be giving her an option. She was pretty sure fighting him on it in front of his men would only make him even more determined. Men liked to be in control. Or at least appear to be. No way she'd win that battle.

She bit her lip.

"The morning, then," she said. "You'll show me the way back home in the morning. Right?"

He lifted her onto the saddle, then jumped up behind her and put his mouth to her ear. "In the morning," he murmured low, as the camel rose to its feet. "I promise, you will not wish to go back."

A shiver of awareness twisted through her insides at the nearness of his body and the deep rumble of his words. The erotic promise lying under them wrapped her in a veil of temptation, and the uneasy feeling in the pit of her stomach got all mixed up with her attraction to him. She felt helpless against the pull. Unable to resist giving in to him.

What was wrong with her?

She tried in vain to stop the sudden trembling in her limbs that whispered she should take her mare and gallop away as far and as fast as she possibly could, no matter how dangerous the wilderness was after sunset. Because she had a sinking feeling that going anywhere with this man, regardless of the time of day, would be far more hazardous to her body and soul than any snakes and scorpions could ever be.

But the steely arm that banded around her midriff told her loud and clear she wouldn't be going anywhere he didn't want her to go. Not tonight, anyway.

She eased out an unsteady breath. Okay. *One night*, she told herself. She could let him have his way for one night. It wasn't like she hadn't already tacitly agreed to it. Or that she didn't want it. Because she did. It made no sense at all, but she wasn't afraid of him that way—not physically, not sexually. His hands on her body were not hard or cruel. Their touch spoke of gentle persuasion and breathtaking skill, not of force.

She would give him tonight. But in the morning… in the morning she was so out of there. No matter how amazingly sexy and tempting the man was.

Because the whole shape-shifting death warrior thing? *That* scared the living daylights out of her.

Chapter 7

Nephtys was terrified to go to sleep.

After the upsetting vision she'd had of surrendering herself to Haru-Re at Petru, she was certain he must have discovered a way to bespell her through her dreams. It was the only explanation—if the vision was a true premonition of the future. Unfortunately, her visions were seldom wrong.

But this one must be! She would never desert Seth-Aziz or Khepesh. Never willingly give herself over to her brother's enemy. To her own betrayer. *Never!*

Ray must have found some insidious way to influence her actions by appearing in her dreams.

She touched the bite marks on her neck and shivered, tamping down the sexual response that coursed through her body at the light touch on her skin. She'd barely slept since his disturbingly erotic nocturnal visits last week, when he'd left his mark on her...in her...

Meruati, he'd whispered seductively as he'd made love to her in her dream. *Come back to me. I need you. I want you here by my side. Come to Petru...*

Lies! All lies!

He didn't want her. But he did need her. Or rather, he needed her magical powers. His numbers at Petru were dwindling, and Nephtys was the only priestess left alive who knew the spell that would grant a human immortality. Ray's seduction was purely self-interest, nothing to do with any tender feelings for her. She knew that.

It mattered not that she was in love with him. Love meant nothing to a man like Haru-Re. Even in her own heart, the line was thin between love and hate.

She squeezed her eyes shut and leaned back among the floor pillows of her meditation room, exhausted. If only she could make it to sunset. Ray was the high priest of the Sun God Re-Horakhti, Guardian of the Morning Light; the chances of his venturing abroad at night were far less than during the day. But she didn't think she could hold out much longer.

What would happen if he came to her again? Would he make her do things, promise things, that would complicate her life even further? Or ruin it altogether? She let out a soft moan of despair.

"Why do you fight me so, *meruati?*"

She gasped and sat up, whirling to the deep rumble of his voice. He lay stretched out among her pillows, his tall, athletic body reposing like a lion at rest. Relaxed, elegant, lethally dangerous.

"Ray!" She scuttled backward, heart pounding. "How did you get in here?"

He regarded her with a mysterious smile. "You invited me."

"I didn't." This was one time she fervently wished the old myth about having to invite a vampire into one's home were true.

She glanced toward the door, wondering what the chances were that she could shift and make it out of the room before he caught her. She loved her sleek feline body, but there were times she wished she had chosen her Set-animal more wisely. A temple cat had few defenses against the likes of one who could become any creature he wished.

"Don't even try," he admonished calmly, as though reading her mind. "Your fluffy kitty is no match for the savage beasts I can call forth. I wouldn't want to hurt you."

Too late, she thought bleakly.

"You needn't shift to be a savage beast, Ray," she retorted.

He chuckled, completely unoffended by the insult. "I am rather magnificently forbidding, aren't I?"

The man's ego was colossal. How she found him the least bit attractive was a mystery for the ages. Except, of course, that he *was* attractive. Unreasonably so.

"What do you want from me?" she ground out, sticking her hands under her armpits to keep him from seeing them shake.

"Oh, I think you know what I want."

In the blink of an eye he was in front of her on his knees, reaching out to pull her body up and into his arms.

"No!" she cried, pushing him away. It took all her strength and willpower. "I don't want you here. I don't want *you*."

"We both know that's not true," he said, the air around him beginning to spark, as it invariably did when his temper piqued. "I've never had to force myself on you, *meruati*. Come. Put aside this distasteful coyness and welcome me properly."

His mouth came down on hers and she groaned in dismay. Her powers were no match for his. Nor was her resolve. She couldn't win this skirmish. *But she had to try.*

She turned her head, breaking the kiss. "Tell me how you got in here and I'll consider your plea."

He wrapped his big hand around the back of her neck and brushed his thumb over the bite marks he'd left on her throat last week. An electric spangle of carnal desire shimmered through her and she let out an unwilling moan. It was a deliberate demonstration of his power over her, she knew that. She also knew she had little defense against him, should he decide to just take what he wanted rather than negotiate.

"An ancient spell," he conceded when she'd all but forfeited the win. "On a scroll long forgotten."

He gazed into her eyes and she forced herself not to look away. Daring him to glamour her. "Then I must find the spell's reversal, mustn't I?"

Slowly he smiled, but didn't take up her gauntlet. "By the Orb, I have missed you, woman," he murmured. "No one else dares talk back or disobey my command. Your bravery excites me. Along with your incredible beauty, of course."

She battled back the seductive effect of his words and scooted away from him. "Odd that it took five thousand years for you to realize such a profound attraction." The bitterness in her observation rang loud and clear.

His lips twitched, his dark eyes following her

as she pulled away and flopped down among the pillows again. He said, "Perhaps it is my two newest initiates who remind me of feelings I have long repressed."

For a microsecond, her heart stalled. Repressed? But that would imply they actually dwelled in his heart, which she knew to be patently false. "You speak of Lord Kilpatrick and Lady Gillian?"

In a graceful movement, Ray eased his tall frame down on his side next to her, head resting on a palm above his bent elbow. Far too close for comfort. "Their love for one another is…inspirational. That they are willing to incur the wrath of a demigod to stay together is a testament to the depth of their devotion."

So they were in Petru. She'd sought a vision of their whereabouts but had not succeeded. Visions were fickle; she knew that only too well. As was devotion…

"More like stupidity," she returned. "Seth is very angry at their defection."

Ray's eyes narrowed. "And yet he has not put a price on their heads. Why is that, I wonder?"

"Because of my vision," she answered, semitruthfully. No doubt they had already told him their reasons for fleeing Khepesh, so lying about that was futile. Better to be straight and not make him suspicious. They wouldn't know of the possible revision to her prophecy. "She is my brother's future consort."

"I rather doubt that," he said, his long fingers toying with the folds of her gown.

"Do not think for a moment we won't get her back," she said, yanking it away from him. "Seth is quite determined." Regardless of her position at the temple.

A dusting of sparkles wafted over his hand. His lashes lowered a fraction. "Perhaps a trade could be arranged. The lady Gillian…for you."

She snorted. "Dream on. It will never happen. Seth-Aziz will never betray me as you did."

Ray's eyes flared, then went flat. "No need. Kilpatrick has become one of my lieutenants and has already shared many of Khepesh's secrets with us. Be wise about your loyalties, my love. It is only a matter of time before I am once again your lord and master, and the one to decide your fate for all eternity."

A shiver worked its way up her spine. To her dismay, it was unclear to her whether it was a shiver of horror…or excitement.

As if in answer, he reached out and ran his fingertips along her cheek and down her throat, again brushing over the bite marks he'd left there. Her addiction flared to life and an agonizing surge of desire swamped through her. This time he didn't let up. Caressing them steadily with his thumb, he slid his fingers around her neck and, oh, so slowly, he leaned over her. As she watched, his fangs lengthened and sharpened. Her heartbeat took off into the stratosphere.

"No," she whispered, but even to herself it sounded like a breathless plea of "yes."

He scraped the loose sleeve of her gown down off her shoulder, leaving her throat, chest and upper arm bare and exposed. He dipped under the wide neckline and found her breast with his palm and cupped it. A surge of want shot through her whole being.

She held her breath, anticipating the touch of his mouth that would send her body into a conflagration of pleasure. But he was a cruel lover and withheld it, holding back for long, endless moments until she thought she would go mad for want of it. Of him. He held his lips over her, a fraction above, never touching her skin, moving with excruciating slowness down to her breast. The warmth of his breath was like the sun on her skin, the suss of her own blood crying to burst free of her veins and into his mouth like a chant in her ears.

Finally, *finally*, he extended his tongue and put the moist tip of it to her breast. She cried out, her body bowing up in blissful want. She pushed her aching nipple into his mouth. He enveloped it and sucked, his fangs piercing her flesh in a sting of pleasure-pain.

She came up off the bed. And detonated in a mind-shattering orgasm. Which was over all too quickly, leaving her just as needy—a mind trick of her addiction for the vampire's kiss. Each climax only enhanced her greed for the next.

He shifted to the other breast, and the agonizing pleasure swept her up into its clutches again. She cried his name and she felt him smile against her flesh. And then she shattered again.

When it was over, their clothes were gone and he was between her thighs, fisting his cock in readiness to come into her.

"Who is your lord and master?" he demanded, his voice gritty with his own need.

She looked up at him, her body screaming for his possession. "Seth-Aziz," she forced herself to answer.

A burst of fireworks exploded above them, showering down in pinpricks of heat on her skin. Angrily, Ray pressed the head of his cock against her slick opening, stopping just short of entrance. She saw stars, her body aching in an agony of want.

"Please," she begged.

His eyes narrowed. "Who is your lord and master, Nephtys? Take care how you answer!"

She swallowed. Hanging on to her will by a thread. "Seth-Aziz!" she croaked past the heart-lump throbbing in her throat.

A crack of lightning lit up the room. Ray's eyes flashed with fury. "I can crush you like a scarab beetle, *meruati*," he growled. "I can burn you with my fire and suck the life from your veins if you do not tell me what I want to hear!"

"Then do it!" she spat out. "Kill me and watch your *shemsu* dwindle and your *per netjer* slowly die! If I am gone, it will be the end of immortality for *all* the ancients! Go on! Drain me of my life! I am past caring," she cried.

But she knew he would not. Could not. His first duty was to his god. Not his ego, as vast as it was.

He would not ask for her allegiance again. Three times said aloud was an unbreakable oath to Seth-Aziz. Ray dare not risk it.

But that did not mean she wouldn't pay for her defiance.

"You will regret this," he ground out. "For I intend to have you! To *own* you. And when you are again my slave, by the rod of Osiris, you shall *not* defy me!"

Bolts of brilliant light strobed from Haru-Re's fingers as they curled into the flesh of her arm and drove into the mass of her hair. His body crushed onto hers, spreading her trembling thighs with his muscular legs. He held her fast, unable to move.

Then his mouth was on her neck. She cried out as his fangs stabbed into her. Amidst a surrounding blaze of dazzling radiance, he plunged his cock deep into her.

And—*may the gods have pity on her*—she rejoiced.

Chapter 8

"Wow. This is what you call a camp?"

At Gemma's fascinated question, Shahin glanced from where they'd paused at the top of the dunes and down to the place he'd called home for the past three-hundred-odd years.

"Why? What would you call it?" he asked, trying to see it through her eyes. Wondering if her impression was a good one or bad one.

The camp was situated in a rare permanent desert oasis, tucked into a narrow, sheltered valley in the midst of the sea of massive dunes, a vivid patch of green grass and tall, elegant palms, flowering plants and rippling pools of crystal-blue water. A few dozen multipeaked nomad tents were scattered along the verdant shore, brightly decorated in patterns of red and blue, with hanging tassels and fluttering pennants. Each tent had an awning that stretched out from the front door, under which mounds of pillows lay scattered about on thick Persian carpets. The porches were arranged facing west, toward the daily battle between darkness and light—the one which darkness always won.

"It looks like something straight out of Burton's *Arabian Nights*," she murmured.

"Does that mean you approve?" he asked, more curious than anything else. Other women he'd brought here had not been so impressed. Not by the camp, at any rate. The awe had come later.

"It's beautiful," she said.

Shahin agreed. And he thought it even more so from the reflected colors of the impending night— reds and oranges like the ripening skins of sweet Nubian grapefruits against the cobalt of the sky.

The woman had once again managed to surprise him.

As his small troop rode into the oasis, they were met by several servants and a handful of smiling women bearing cups of water. After they dismounted, Shahin accepted two cups and passed one to Gemma.

"Cut the dust with this, and then we shall have

cocktails as we watch the nightfall," he told her. The sun was nearing the horizon, and it was custom in camp to watch the golden arc in its daily defeat by the power of the Lord of Night.

He drank down his water in a gulp, tossed his *bisht* and turban to one of the servants, then called over to a boy standing nearby. "Take care of madam's horse," he instructed. "You know what to do, yes?"

"Yes, my lord!" The boy ran off, a grin on his face to have been so entrusted.

"Cocktails?" Gemma asked, brow raised, as he led her over to a large tent.

"There is no sharia law here," he said, running his fingers through his hair. "We keep the old ways, with no proscription against alcohol. In any case, I am Coptic, not Muslim."

She tipped her head in puzzlement. "You're Christian? Not a follower of Set-Sutekh, as the Shahin legend says?"

So he was still being tested.

"I am, indeed, one of the *shemsu*, a follower. And I am a Christian as well," he returned, and invited her to sit with him under his front canopy. "I see no contradiction." He arranged a pile of pillows behind his back and stretched out his legs. It was good to be home. "This is Egypt, a land where—"

But Gemma wasn't listening. She was gaping

at the camels—what was left of them. They were slowly dissolving, swirling like mist into thin air.

"They are ghost camels," he explained, reminding himself this was all new to her. "Not real."

She blinked. "But…but we were just riding them! They were solid and…"

"Conjured. It comes in handy when one must shift back to human form unexpectedly, as today. We are immortal, but twenty miles on foot across the desert is not my idea of a pleasant afternoon stroll."

She swallowed. And dropped abruptly down onto the pillows next to him. She ran a hand over her eyes, and he could see her fingers were shaking a little. "This is insane."

She drew a deep breath and looked him in the eyes. "You really *are* what you say. Aren't you?" But it wasn't a question, but more of a rasped statement of reluctant acceptance. Finally.

"Yes," he said. "It is true."

Just then, the servant reappeared carrying a drinks tray, and another with a low brass table, which were arranged on the rug between him and Gemma. Then the servants bowed and melted away. Shahin picked up the pitcher, poured a splash of pinkish liquid into two stemmed glasses and handed her one. "Here. You'll feel better after a few sips."

"Martinis?" she asked, looking at the time-honored shape of the glasses half-amused, half-incredulous.

He smiled and shrugged, settling back to watch the drama unfolding before them. The glowing golden ball of the sun was just disappearing behind the crest of the highest dune, the air around it shimmering with the dying heat of the day. Fingers of indigo darkness stretched across the sky, reaching, reaching to snuff out the dimming light as it had for an eternity, and would for another.

He lifted his glass in a toast. "What can I say. I had a good British friend who was a very bad influence."

She frowned, noticing the faint color of the drink, caused by a handful of red seeds slowly sinking to the bottom of the glass. "I thought martinis were supposed to have olives," she said.

"Not mine. Taste," he urged.

She sipped, tipping a few seeds into her mouth and rolling them on her tongue. Suddenly her eyes flared, and he could see her struggle to decide whether to spit them out or not. She finally swallowed, and said, "Seriously? Pomegranate seeds? That's not a bit obvious?"

He smiled, pleased that she'd caught the irony. "Don't worry, *kalila*. I assure you, I am not Hades. I simply like the taste of pomegranate."

And unlike Persephone, there would be no

bargains made for her freedom. He was hers. Not for six months of the year, but for as long as he wished to keep her.

She took another sip; this time, her swallow was more convulsive. She glanced sideways at the ragged silhouette of tents that stretched the length of the valley, then westward, to the giant dunes that rolled out from the oasis, stretching halfway across the continent of Africa. The orange sun was nearly gone now, consumed by the deepening darkness of the coming night. Just a sliver remained, hovering like a burning drop of mercury on the horizon.

She watched it as she said, "You aren't planning to let me go in the morning, are you."

Again, not a question.

She was still bespelled, but only concerning her attraction to him, not regarding her capture. Apparently, that would be unnecessary, it seemed, even for the short term. He was glad she'd accepted her fate. It would make everything so much easier on her.

"No," he affirmed. "I am not."

The last remnant of sun blinked out, vanquished. She did not look back at him.

"Why?" she asked quietly. "Why me?"

He sensed she did not want to be given platitudes, told he'd taken her because she was the most beautiful woman in the world and he couldn't live another day without having her. She wanted the truth. The strange thing was, that *was* the truth. Or part of it, at least. If she hadn't thoroughly captured his masculine interest at the temple yesterday, she would now be a prisoner in Khepesh, awaiting the decision of the high priest as to what would be done with her.

Being here with him was infinitely better. Here, she would have a chance to learn what it was like to be an immortal in the service of the god, and could decide to join the *per netjer* of her own free will. For if she didn't, she would be robbed of that free will and turned into a *shabti*, a human servant, to spend eternity in the service of the immortals, with no trace of her former self intact. A living purgatory.

The unhappy fate of his own mother.

He shook off the unwelcome reminder of his family and tamped down the instinctive fury that always rode him just beneath the surface because of it, consuming him with the need for revenge.

"It's complicated," he said gruffly, and jerked down the remainder of his martini, then poured another and topped up hers.

"It would appear," she said drily, "that I have nothing but time on my hands. So go ahead. Give me the unabridged version."

He sighed and silently debated what and how much to tell her this early on. But he was not a palace courtier used to prevarication and intrigue. He was a warrior, for better or worse, plainspoken and straightforward. So he gave her the no-frills version.

"Actually," he said, "it's your sister we want. You are just...shall we say, collateral damage."

She stared at him. "Excuse me?"

"I'm speaking of the *per netjer*, the temple, of course. Not me personally. Because you are definitely the sister I want. *Only* you." He gave her a smile. But he saw plainly it did not take the bite from his words.

She opened her mouth, then closed it again. "I don't understand," she said at length. "Why does the cult, this *per netjer* as you call it, want my sister? *Which* sister?"

He adjusted his position on the pillows, turning toward her somberly. "At first, it was Gillian. Somehow, she discovered the hidden entrance to Khepesh Palace, the home of the immortals of Set-Sutekh. You must understand, there was no way we could let her leave with that knowledge."

Gemma frowned. "Gillian is a historian and she'd been hired to find some long-lost British lord's grave. She was out searching for it on the day she vanished. But she phoned us. She told us she'd met a man and had decided to stay with him for a while."

She leveled Shahin a gaze. "Are you saying that wasn't true?"

He shook his head. "No, that much was indeed true. It was Lord Kilpatrick she met. He is…was… one of us."

Gemma's eyes widened and for a moment she was mute. Then, "My God. *Lord Rhys Kilpatrick?* It was *his* grave Gillian was searching for! But he's been dead for over a hundred y—" Her sentence choked off in dismay.

"Needless to say, Kilpatrick is still very much alive," Shahin said. "And in love with your sister. They ran away together."

Gemma closed her eyes and amazed him when her lips lifted in a bleak smile. "Thank God. At least something good has come out of all this insanity. She mentioned a wedding in her note. So they eloped?"

At the reminder of Rhys's treachery, Shahin finished his drink with a scowl and set the glass on the brass table with a clunk. Seth claimed to have himself engineered Rhys's defection to Petru, the palace of their enemy, as a sort of Trojan horse, but Shahin feared Seth's fondness for the Englishman had convinced him of a loyalty that did not exist. "Not exactly," he said.

"What happened?" she asked.

"Our priestess, Nephtys, had a vision of Gillian as

the demigod Seth-Aziz's consort. The wedding she mentioned was to Seth, not Kilpatrick. But she and Rhys defied the god and went over to our enemy, Haru-Re, to seek sanctuary."

Gemma's jaw dropped. "You can't be serious. You wanted her to be consort to a demigod?" Her expression turned to patent disbelief. She started to shake her head, then shot him a sharp glance. "Wait. Seth-Aziz? As in Seth-Aziz the high priest of the cult of *Set-Sutekh?* The one in all the local native legends? *That's* the cult you're talking about?"

"Cult has such a negative connotation. You must use the term *per netjer.* Ours is not a cult worshiping a specific deity. It's a way of life. An offering of service."

But again she was not listening. She looked completely aghast. "But Seth-Aziz, he's supposed to be a…a…"

"Vampire?" he helpfully supplied. "Yes, he is."

"No…" she whispered, going deathly pale. "Vampires don't exist." Her denials were getting repetitious.

"They do. Two of them, at any rate. Haru-Re our enemy, and Seth-Aziz, our leader."

"And you wanted my sister to be his consort." She looked utterly appalled.

"We still do. Well, one of them."

"You can't be serious. Surely, you don't mean…?"

Shahin jetted out a decisive breath. "Oh, but that's exactly what I mean. Seth has decided that because of Lady Gillian's defection, your other sister, Josslyn, is to take her place. As his wife."

"No!" Gemma jumped up so fast that the rest of her drink splashed out of the glass, soaking her shirt. She barely noticed. "How *dare* you?" she demanded. "What gives you the right to force such a thing on her? On *any* woman? Did it ever occur to you that she might not want to be a vampire's— His—"

"Don't," Shahin warned, and rose in a single swift motion.

He grasped her arms when she whirled and started to stalk off. Where she'd go, she had no idea. But it didn't matter. This was too much. "Let go of me!"

"There's one thing you need to understand," he growled. "We don't force ourselves on anyone. In fact, we go to great lengths to avoid mortals even knowing of our existence. It was Gillian who intruded on our space and forced our hand. But in the end, she chose to join us and agreed to become Seth's consort of her own free will."

"I don't believe you!" Gemma spat out. "Consort to a *vampire?*"

"Seth is a demigod, our high priest. Being a

vampire makes him more powerful, but to all appearances, he is a man like any other."

She couldn't decide if he was serious or just plain crazy. So she grabbed on to an objection he couldn't argue against. "Even if what you say is true—and I don't believe it for a second—she wouldn't leave Joss and me like that. With no explanation." *Just as their mother had…*

"What would you have had her say?" Shahin argued. "In any event, she did phone you and wrote the note so you wouldn't worry. But believe me, she intended to stay. She wants to be with us." He tugged her closer to his body. "Just as you will."

She didn't think so. Shahin might not be planning to let her go in the morning, but she had no intention of staying. Hello? She wanted nothing to do with a cult of vampires! Shahin wasn't *that* sexy.

Besides, he wasn't interested in her anyway. She was just *collateral damage.*

She tried to block him out, but his otherworldly energy, potent and shiveringly seductive, spilled through her, weakening her resistance. Her breasts tingled, and a rash of goose bumps splashed over her arms where his fingers touched her. Okay, maybe he was that sexy. But Sheikh Shahin was far too dangerous to mess with. This whole thing was dangerous and insane. She had to warn Joss.

She tried to pull away, knowing if she didn't,

she'd be lost. "We're not talking about me," she insisted. "Or even Gillian. But Josslyn. Vampire or no, no one can make her marry a man she's not in love with!"

"It's not my decision, *kalila*. And from what I've seen, your sister is more than capable of taking care of herself and making her own decisions."

"Yes, but—"

"Seth is very angry right now, but as I've told you, he is not a monster. I'm sure he will listen to her if she objects."

"If?"

His tension gave way to a lazy, bone-melting smile. Watching the change in demeanor from captor to seducer, her whole body tingled.

"Seth-Aziz is a very powerful and charming man," Shahin said. "I'm sure he will persuade her of his…many attractions." He paused to let his gaze drift slowly down her body, then started to walk her backward into the tent. "And perhaps, my dear, it is time to persuade you of mine."

Alarm buzzed through her. Along with an unwanted wash of intense arousal. Heavens. What was *wrong* with her? "Shahin—"

"I like how you say my name, *kalila*," he murmured, parting the curtained door behind her with a hand and kept backing her up.

She struggled to keep her wits about her as she

was enveloped by the cool dimness of the tent—and a thick fog of awareness. His endearment echoed in her heart like a love song. *Kalila*. She really wished he would stop calling her that. It was messing with her will to stay strong.

"I'm not your sweetheart," she croaked, pushing at his chest. But he was immovable. Like the Sphinx. "Are you a vampire, too?" she asked, terrified of the answer.

"No. Just Seth-Aziz."

Thank God! Her heart spun with relief. And something else.

"Worried?"

"What do you think?" She tried to wriggle from his grasp. It was no use.

His warm breath stirred her hair. "Why do you fight me?" he murmured. "You know we both want this."

Maybe she did want him, physically. There was no denying it. But…if she gave herself over to him, what was she really consenting to? A brief fantasy affair…or to spend forever in some mythical cult she didn't believe in?

She licked her lips, desperately seeking a way to delay what seemed more and more inevitable. "I do want you, Shahin. But…I'm…I'm covered in martini and dust, and—"

He stilled and his expression turned wry. "Ah,

I understand. The desert heat. My smell offends you."

"No, you smell wonderful. It's just—" She knew she'd made a tactical error when that lazy smile reappeared. *Damn.*

"All the same, what kind of a gentleman would I be not to offer my lady a soothing bath after a hard day of riding?"

He didn't add. "and before indulging in a ride of a different sort," but it was plainly written in the slant of his dark, languorous eyes.

She pulled at her martini-soaked shirt, pretending she didn't understand exactly what he was saying. "That would be, um, great."

"Excellent. Come with me."

If she'd expected him to call a bevy of servants to pull out a copper tub and heat water to fill it, giving her an hour or more to debate her options, she was sadly mistaken.

He lifted her knuckles to his lips and kissed them, then linked fingers and led her through another curtained door in the very back of the tent. "Here we are."

Her breath caught. They'd entered a smaller tent that was attached to the main one like a satellite. But this room had a tile floor instead of carpets, and contained an elaborate stone basin, like a Roman tub, fed by a bubbling hot spring that cascaded over the lip in a smooth, wide fall. A light mist of sweetly fragrant steam rose invitingly from the water, curling into the gauzy lengths of shimmery fabric that decorated the inside walls of the tent. The whole room had an air of sensual mystery.

He waved his hand and a hundred glowing flames sprang to life, lighting the drifts of candles that were scattered about on the stone surfaces.

Instantly, her qualms were forgotten. "Oh! It's lovely!" She went to the edge of the tub and dipped her fingers in. The temperature was perfect. She sighed in delight. The bathroom in the rental villa was primitive, the shower an ugly cement cubicle. She turned to tell him how much she was going to enjoy this.

And her breath caught again, this time for an entirely different reason.

He'd taken off his tunic, peeled down to his bare skin.

His chest was magnificent, broad and lean and olive tan. His abs were a rippling six-pack, all angled shadows, bisected by a light vee of black hair.

He walked over to the basin, sat down on the rim, and pulled off his riding boots. First one, then the other, hit the floor. "What are you waiting for, *kalila*?"

She blinked. *Oh, lord.*

"You want to…" She glanced at the swirling

water as he poured a handful of crystals into it and they began to foam. "Together?"

His brows rose. "That's generally how it's done. Unless you Americans have invented a new way I'm unfamiliar with?"

He obviously wasn't talking about bathing.

He untied the waistband of his trousers. They, too, dropped to the floor.

Leaving him completely, wonderfully, rampantly naked.

Not what she'd expected.

But oh. My. God.

Impossible to refuse.

Chapter 9

Ribbons of heat shot through Gemma from the roots of her hair to the tips of her toes. *Mine*, she thought giddily. *All mine*.

"Shy?" Shahin asked when she didn't—*couldn't*—move. He came toward her. "Shall I undress you?"

"N-no," she stammered. "I mean y-yes." She slammed her eyes shut. Totally befuddled and embarrassed. "I mean—"

"Shh," he murmured, reaching for her. "It's okay. I will bare your body for you."

She stood immobile, helpless to move. Her blood was thick with want and her limbs trembled with need as he, one by agonizing one, unfastened the buttons of her shirt. He pushed it from her shoulders, leaned in and brushed the tip of his nose along the side of her temple, burrowing into her hair, rubbing his cheek against hers in an impossibly sensual gesture. Not quite affection, not quite possessive, but something in-between.

Her shirt fell to the floor, and his lips moved down her throat, trailing along her collarbone and across her shoulder, leaving sparks of unbearable desire along the way.

He unhooked her bra and tossed it aside. When it was in midair he made a movement with his fingers and it disintegrated in a short burst of flame and smoke. Then his hands were on her naked breasts.

She gasped as he cupped them and flicked his thumbs across her nipples, as he had when they were on the camel. An excruciating need flamed through her. He teased and squeezed her until she thought she would go mad. She couldn't take this much longer.

"Please," she softly begged. "I want you."

"I know," he murmured, shifting to unfasten her riding breeches and inch them down over her hips. "I have bespelled you."

Her mind was too dizzy from his touch to truly grasp what he was saying. "Yes," she agreed on a soft, desperate moan. "I am completely under your spell."

He lowered himself to his knees in front of her and drew off her boots, and in a twinkling, the rest of her clothes. When she was as nude as he, he gazed up at her. His black eyes burned with…she didn't know, but whatever the emotion, it was strong and fierce. And a little frightening.

Make that downright scary. Because the intensity of it only made her want him more.

How crazy was that?

He put his hands on her and ran them slowly, deliberately, over the flesh of her curves. She was ready to detonate. She wanted him on top of her, *in* her. Swallowing her up with his incredible sensual power.

He rose to his feet and cupped her face in his large hands. She could feel the barely leashed strength of his fingers as he caressed her jaw. She shivered.

"Please," she whispered.

"No, I will not take you like this," he said.

Confusion bewildered what was left of her brain. "I…I don't understand."

"You are bespelled. Unable to say no. There is no honor in possessing a woman like that. It brings no real pleasure, for either of us."

She begged to disagree.

Shaking her head, she reached for him. She

needed to feel his body against hers, skin to skin, his thick arousal completing her, filling her. Yes, *possessing* her. Her flesh ached for it. For him.

"Believe me, I don't want to say no," she assured.

"That's because I took away your will to deny me. Yesterday, when I saw you at the temple, I put a spell of passion on you, and again last night in your dreams. It was essential you come to me, and the easiest way to accomplish that was to make you want me as a lover. I gave you no choice in the matter."

Her *dreams?* Memories of the erotic dreams she'd had of him washed through her mind and body.

If she weren't so weak with unfulfilled need, she might be insulted. Her desire for him was as real as it got. Their attraction was strong and mutual. Not the result of some kind of voodoo magic. Or dreams.

"Wanting you was *not* why I came looking for you today," she began, then paused for a reality check. "All right, maybe it was, but that was only part of the reason." Unfortunately, she couldn't remember what the other part was at the moment. "Wanting you was just…" She faltered. What *was* it? Other than complete insanity? She licked her lips. "…a fantasy."

He kissed her then. A deep, drowning kiss. And

said, "I hope I fulfill it. But I'm going to lift the spell now, so be prepared. Your true feelings about the fantasy may be…other than you think."

Before she could really comprehend what he was saying—or doing—he moved his hand in front of her and said a few indecipherable words. She blinked, waiting for something to happen. For her burning need for him to lessen or evaporate.

It didn't.

She didn't feel any different at all. Just the same incredible attraction. The same dizzying want. The same overwhelming need to feel his body touching hers.

"I still want you," she said, and pressed herself up against him. Frustrated from waiting. Breathless with anticipation.

Slowly, he smiled and gathered her close. "Good. Because I don't know if I could have stopped myself from taking you."

With that, he swept her up into his arms and carried her over to the bath. He stepped in and let her slide down his body until her feet touched bottom. The water was deep, past her knees. It was deliciously warm and effervescent. Cascades of foam bubbles tickled her calves. The spicy fragrance of the crystals he'd added rose in intoxicating drifts.

His mouth came down on hers. Desire roared over her, stronger than ever. She lost all sense of everything but him. His heat, his touch, his scent were all she knew.

Together, they sank down into the water, their kiss a living thing. Deep and intense, wet and thorough. Her heart pounded. Her body quickened and blossomed. Oh, how she wanted him!

"Shahin," she whispered, and he gave a little groan, pulling her onto his lap. She wrapped her legs around his waist, straddling his thighs, loving how he crushed her body to his. She could feel his arousal, thick and long, pressed intimately against her. And she knew he wanted her as much as she wanted him.

"I don't want to wait any longer," she murmured. She lifted up, inviting him to thrust in.

"No," he growled, and banded an arm around her hips, pulling her back down onto his lap. But unjoined. "Not yet."

She groaned in frustration. "Why? Another spell?"

"This one you'll like."

He drove his fingers through her hair and wound it around his fist, tipping her head back. He kissed her again, thrusting his tongue deep, deep into her mouth. He lapped at her and sucked.

"Oh!" She gasped at an unexpected shock of sensation between her thighs. It felt like his mouth was on her there. *There*. Exactly where she wanted him. He laved her mouth again, and she nearly detonated.

"Good?" he asked, low and rough.

"Mmm," was all she could manage. How did he *do* that?

He suckled her tongue as she tried to catch the breath that had stalled in her throat. Pleasure flamed through her center. Her body bowed in his arms.

"Yes," she moaned. "Oh, yes."

He kept at it, making her writhe and pant in electric pleasure, taking her higher and higher until she cried out and came apart in his arms in the most intense climax she'd ever experienced. As her body quaked and shook with the force of her pleasure, the earth literally moved. Water splashed out of the tub in waves. Candles around the room toppled and sputtered out. The gauzy curtains rippled and swayed. He rolled with her until she reclined under him in the water.

"Ohhh," she moaned as he released his mouth from hers and gazed down at her with glittering eyes. "That was…*amazing*."

"We've barely gotten started, *kalila*," he murmured huskily.

She didn't think she could move, so she just lay back and enjoyed his ministrations as he washed her body and hair. "You have wonderful hands," she told him, closing her eyes. She could get used to this.

"You have a beautiful body," he returned, his touch growing more intimate.

She smiled. And spread her legs for him.

"Are you a virgin?"

Surprised, she popped her eyes open. He didn't meet her gaze. "Um, no."

There was a sharp rumbling and a few more candles tipped over. She grabbed the rim of the tub, looking around in alarm. "What *is* that? An earthquake?"

"Yes," he said, his voice tight. "Earthquakes are my element to call. Sometimes it happens when I am excited. But more often, when I am provoked."

She wasn't sure what to think—about either part of his confession. She picked the easier, but possibly more disturbing issue. "You're angry I'm not a virgin?"

His head gave a small shake. "No, not angry. Perhaps disappointed."

His chauvinism was like a dash of cold water. "Shahin, you can't have it both ways. If I were a virgin, I wouldn't be here with you. I'd be safe at home waiting for a wedding band."

"Oh, you'd be here," he refuted in a gravelly, masculine growl that made her shiver. He dunked his head backward to rinse his hair in the falling stream of water. So damn sure of himself she wanted to strangle the man.

This was not exactly how the fantasy was supposed to go. So while he was rinsing, she got up and stepped out of the bath. She glanced around for a towel.

The water roared and he came up out of it like an avenging god. In less than a second he'd grasped her arms in an iron grip. "Where do you think you're going?"

Despite the absurdity of the situation, a prick of hurt lanced through her chest. She lifted her chin. "I wouldn't want to be a disappointment to you, Shahin."

"Don't be ridiculous," he ground out, water streaming in silver runnels down his hard body. "Of course you're not." Behind her, a vase crashed to the floor.

She jumped, eyeing it. "Why don't I believe you?"

His mouth thinned but he didn't let her go. "I was born at a time when such things mattered, Gemma. I know better now. I promise. But sometimes it just comes flying out of nowhere. I'm sorry."

He seemed so sincere she almost believed him. Almost.

His gaze drilled into hers. "I chose you, *kalila*. You could never disappoint me."

For a split second she felt herself melting again. Except…then she remembered. He *hadn't* chosen her. She'd simply landed in his sexual crosshairs because the demigod he worked for apparently preferred blondes.

Which was probably better than the alternative. But not terribly convincing of his genuine interest in her.

"Come to bed," he murmured, putting his lips to her forehead. He soothed his hands down her arms. "Let me prove how much I want you. How little I care about your other lovers."

His hands snaked around to her bottom and gently squeezed as he pressed her closer, center to center.

Okay, so a certain part of his interest was undeniably genuine. And convincing. *Very* convincing.

She shouldn't give in to him so easily, but she couldn't help herself. She still wanted him, chauvinist and all. "I suppose I could pretend to be a virgin," she said with a moue.

"By Mithra's balls, no!" he said exasperated, and scowled. "I want you just the way you are."

She smiled. So maybe he *could* be taught. "In that case," she said, twining her arms around his neck, "I may just let you have me."

Chapter 10

Shahin was thoroughly captivated. Gemma was an inspiring lover.

Stretching awake, he glanced over at her sprawled on the bed in sexy disarray, her pale, shapely limbs in pleasing contrast to the black satin linens, her hair a cloud of auburn strewn across the pillows, half obscuring her pretty face.

He'd been agreeably surprised by her.

Rarely did women hold his interest for more than a time or two—after all, how many ways could you join with a woman without it becoming mindless, empty physicality—in other words, boring? But Gemma had kept him aroused and coming back for more the whole night long. She was open and mischievous, curious and seductive, and so damned trusting of him that he actually thought his passion spell had somehow not been lifted, and when she dropped off for a few minutes he'd repeated the incantation to reverse it again. But when she opened her eyes, she'd just looked up at him with that same misty, romantic look in them.

He wanted to shake her until her teeth rattled and tell her not to be so bloody naive. He did not trust her; she sure as hell should not trust him.

He would use her and then let her go, as he invariably did with all women. Tender feelings did not enter into his plans. Not with her. Not with any woman. How could they, after the cruel lesson he'd endured at deceitful female hands? Gemma should keep her emotions to herself and not waste them on a man who had no use for such things.

Still, she was unquestionably a breath of fresh air in his all-too-predictable bed. Women tended to fall into two categories with him: those who were terrified of his powers, and those who were greedy for the things his powers could give them. Neither appealed.

But Gemma seemed determined to forget Sheikh Shahin the immortal, and simply made love with Shahin the man. She delighted when he touched her, laughed when he whispered silly things in her ear, shook in explosive response when he made her come. She gave as good as she got, and demurred at nothing he suggested they try.

And he had suggested many things. Things he hadn't done in ages. Things he hadn't wanted to do with any other woman.

Yes, she was as captivating as one of Isis's famed temple handmaidens. A guileless odalisque. An innocent temptress.

He just might have to keep her around for a good long while. Longer than he'd indicated to Seth. And as the captain of the guard, in charge of keeping the *per netjer* safe from treachery inside and out, possibly longer than was prudent to keep the sister of a traitor.

She stirred and gave a soft hum and a little smile, as though she were dreaming of him. His heart caught.

Followed swiftly by a slap of irritation. He didn't like that she could cause him to drop his guard for even a moment. With a sharp exhale, he slid out of bed and strode to the bath to clean up and get dressed. There were still several hours of nighttime left and he had things to do.

Leaving his tent, he went straight to the stables to check on Gemma's little mare. "See to it she is well cared for," he told the boy, Hasim, whom he'd tasked with the job. "And be sure she does not get loose. Horses have an unerring sense of direction, and she would run straight home."

"Causing unwanted panic over madam," Hasim filled in, nodding. Smart boy.

Hasim was a mortal, one of an endless series of orphan boys whom Shahin had taken in over the years and employed as servants in the camp. As they grew to manhood, some became spies for him in the outside world, some given a pot of money and urged into a suitable profession helpful to the *per netjer*. A few chose to become immortal and join Shahin's Guardians of Khepesh. All were fanatically loyal to him personally. And amply rewarded for that loyalty.

"Exactly," Shahin said, ruffled his hair, then reached out to stroke the horse's muzzle. Having a real animal in camp was rare, other than those they used as food. "Ride her if you wish, come daylight. She'd like the exercise, I'm sure."

Hasim's eyes lit up. "Yes, sir!"

Shahin took his leave, striding out into the night, gathering his cloak around him. With a swift twist of his feet and a soft chant of magical words, his body spun in on itself and became the powerful black hawk of legend. His arms morphed into mighty wings that spread wide on the wind and carried him up into the vast, star-spangled sky.

He circled the oasis once, twice, his sharp avian

eyes scanning the camp to see that all was as it should be.

The guards were posted. A few fires crackled in stony pits, several of his men and a handful of the camp women gathered around each bright blaze, conversing and laughing as they swapped stories and made plans for the next evening's sortie.

All was well.

Yet Shahin's animal instincts took over and he felt suddenly tense. On edge. Something uneasy hovered in the air—a gathering of energy, a premonition, a brush of magic.

But there was nothing wrong that he could see. He shook off the feeling and with a piercing call down to his men, he flew off into the night toward Khepesh.

When he reached the hidden entrance at the very top of the remotest part of the *gebel*, he spoke the unlocking spell in his mind and the entrance yawned open for him. He flew down the stairs and through the midnight-dark tunnels to the Great Western Gate, where he winged to a halt, wheeled in a circle and shifted back to his human form, landing on his feet at the base of the magnificent silver double portal to the palace.

After speaking briefly with the portal guards, telling them to be on extra alert, he went to find Seth-Aziz.

He found him in his private quarters, reading. Unusual…

"My lord," Shahin said, sweeping a bow as he studied his leader's reclining form, "I trust you are well?"

Seth waved him off and set aside the book. "Just a bit tired." He rose and went over to a silver samovar on a sideboard. "Tea?"

"Thanks." Shahin watched him pour the thick black concentrate from a small, ornate kettle over sugar cubes in two tall glasses, then fill them with hot water from the samovar. The strong fragrant aroma tickled his nose as he accepted it and took a grateful sip. He and Gemma had managed to squeeze in a quick meal amidst their bedplay, but they'd not bothered with after-dinner coffee. They'd been too distracted by lust.

"I see by your expression you have something to report," Seth said, settling comfortably onto a silk divan, glass saucer on his knee.

Shahin paced to a copper brazier that blazed in one corner of the room and stared into the flames. "Haru-Re continues to post his guards along our frontier. Our spies are convinced he is readying himself for action against us."

"Not unexpected," Seth remarked, sipping. "Last week he warned us if we didn't agree to share Nephtys with Petru, it would mean war."

"And yet we do nothing," Shahin said, turning in frustration. "I do not have a good feeling about this. We must answer his moves with our own!"

"What would you have me do?" Seth asked calmly. "We do not have the numbers to defeat him in battle. We know it. He knows it. I must resort to other means to quell his threats."

Shahin blew a breath through his nose. "You speak of Lord Kilpatrick." Seth's plan to use his former master steward as a kind of Trojan horse—something he'd inexplicably neglected to tell the man in question—had been a huge bone of contention between them since Kilpatrick and his lover defected to Petru last week. "I cannot believe you would leave the fate of Khepesh in the hands of—"

"No," Seth interrupted. "I am hopeful Rhys will help our cause from inside Haru-Re's stronghold, but I do not depend on him."

"What, then?"

Seth smiled. "Superior strategy."

Shahin hiked a brow, polishing off his tea and setting the glass aside.

Seth shrugged. "Sounds better than fervent prayer and a lot of luck," he said philosophically.

This attitude did not bode well. "You cannot give up, my lord. We all depend upon your strength and wisdom to get us through this crisis."

"I have no intention of giving up. But—" he sighed "—I am…tired."

Shahin straightened, suddenly understanding. "You need blood."

"I'll admit I'm starting to feel the delay of the ceremony." He regarded Shahin somberly. "You must fetch the sisters today so I can feed at once."

"Sister," he corrected, nodding with purpose. This was good. "I already have Gemma Haliday at my camp."

It was Seth's turn to raise his brows. "Indeed? Were you so hungry for the taste of her you couldn't wait?"

Despite the gravity of the situation, Shahin felt his lips curve. "She was the hungry one. She sought me out yesterday, riding into the western desert on her own to search for our oasis."

Seth's grin turned lopsided. "I'm surprised you are here."

"Surprised, why?" asked Nephtys as she breezed into the room and sized them up with a single glance. "Ah, a woman, I gather. Who is it this week, my lord sheikh?"

"Miss Haliday," Seth answered for him, sounding amused as well as mildly impressed. "Gemma, that is. She went to the oasis all on her own."

Nephtys gazed at Shahin consideringly. "Interesting. Did she come for you, or her missing sister?"

"Both," he answered. "But she will stay for me."

"No ego there," Nephtys said, and poured herself a glass of tea. "I assume there is a spell involved?"

"Not at the moment."

"That *is* impressive. *Mabruk*, Shahin. Perhaps you have finally found a woman who will put up with your foul temper and moody disposition." She winked to soften her words, and added a dollop of milk to her tea.

"Amusing as always," he said drily. Nephtys was the one woman in the world he trusted enough to let tease him with impunity. "But it will do her no good to 'put up with me.' I am not interested in keeping her."

"One day," Nephtys said sagely, "you will have to set aside your need to punish all women for the evil deeds of one, Sheikh Shahin."

"Not until my enemy has paid that debt with his life," he returned emphatically. He did not like being reminded of the reason for his defensive posture toward females.

She stirred her tea and regarded him. "You are all about fate and following one's path, are you not, Shahin? Have you not considered that maybe this is the woman meant to join you on that path? Your soul mate?"

He also did not like having his spiritual beliefs

used against him. Though the priestess knew very well he did not believe in forever mates. "No," he said. "I have not."

But then he suddenly wondered if Nephtys had received a vision about him. Not that he would ever ask. He did accept her gift as real, but like a soon-to-be father who refused to speculate about the gender of his coming offspring, Shahin did not want to know what the future held. It was already written, decided long before his birth, and there was nothing he could do but follow his convictions and accept what befell him with honor. Knowing? It only complicated matters. Just look at the hoops Seth was jumping through to fulfill the prophecy of a wise and beloved consort.

But far from condemning Shahin's stance on women, Nephtys, he knew, understood. Perhaps better than most. Had not her own cruel betrayal caused her to eschew men—and love—for all these long millennia? Thank Osiris the fulfillment of his own need for revenge would also discharge hers. He'd hate to think by killing Haru-Re he would be hurting her.

Though the gods knew it wouldn't stop him.

In an unexpected move, she came over to him and placed a warm kiss on his cheek accompanied by a heartfelt sigh. "I truly envy your conviction,

Lord Shahin, and hope the universe grants you the path you imagine."

But something in her voice made him doubt she believed it would be what he expected. *Did* she know something he didn't? His heart stilled, and he thought suddenly of the woman waiting in his bed for him to return. *Was* she somehow tangled up in his destiny?

No. He refused to believe it. Gemma was just a passing dalliance, that was all. A temporary delight. A reward from Set-Sutekh for all his hard work.

He smiled at Nephtys and lifted her knuckles to his lips. "You are most gracious, my lady. I hope the same for you."

"Hey, what about me?" Seth cut in, pretending to appear piqued but failing miserably. Nephtys always brought out the softer side of her autocratic brother.

Shahin glanced at her, but she had already turned away. She went to Seth and settled next to him on the divan. Her smile faltered as she studied her brother's face. "*Hadu*, you look exhausted. Is it the lack of blood?" When he nodded, she said, "You must accept a sacrifice immediately."

He nodded again. "I've already instructed Shahin to fetch Josslyn Haliday to Khepesh today."

"That could take hours. Perhaps days. Let me

send one of my *shemats* to you right away to tide you over."

Seth needed mortal blood, taken from a willing female, to fulfill his obligation to the goddess Sekhmet and renew his strength. But in a pinch, an immortal woman's blood would do to stave off the hunger until an appropriate sacrificial vessel could be found.

He frowned. "God, no. The last thing I need to deal with right now is a vamp-struck temple maiden."

Despite the seriousness of the situation, Shahin smiled. The last time Seth had taken blood from one of the *shemsu*, she'd gotten all starry-eyed, mooning after him for weeks until the euphoria wore off, totally besotted. It took a strong woman to resist a vampire's sexual powers.

"But we need you strong, my brother. You must not succumb to the blood weakness now, of all times," Nephtys argued.

"I'll be fine for a day or two. I wish to wait for my consort. The hungrier I am, the tighter the binding with her. That is my decision."

A lot was riding on the Haliday woman. Shahin hoped she wasn't as hostile and aggressive as she'd seemed at the temple ruin two days ago. "What if she doesn't want any part of it? Or of you?" Shahin asked Seth cautiously. In this instance, he agreed with Nephtys. "We need her acquiescence, and frankly, Josslyn Haliday didn't strike me as the accommodating type."

Two sets of eyes peered at him, one blithely unworried, the other more guarded.

"Then I shall have to employ all my powers of persuasion on her, shan't I?" Seth said. "As will you. How do you propose to gain her consent to bring her here?"

"Both her sisters have gone missing, as well as her mother," Shahin said. "I doubt it will take much convincing to get her to Khepesh of her own free will. Yours will be the more difficult task by far."

"We shall see," Seth said, rising. "In the meantime, keep a close eye on Haru-Re and let me know of any developments on that front. I look forward to your swift return with my future consort, my friend."

"My will is to serve, my lord."

As Shahin left Khepesh Palace, shifted to hawk and took wing aboveground into a darkness that was already beginning to fade, he gauged he had another hour or so before dawn. He decided to make a quick circuit of the slice of desert that Set-Sutekh ruled, the area Shahin was responsible for keeping safe. To prove he was not a slave to his desire for the woman who awaited him in his bed.

Which he wasn't. Not by any means.

His body wanted her, yes. But that would diminish quickly enough. With familiarity she would lose her unique appeal, and his instinctive distrust would eclipse any affection he might have begun to feel for her. It always happened.

Thank Osiris's wisdom, because Shahin didn't know what he'd do if he started wanting a woman for more than a passing fancy. That would be unacceptable. He knew only too well what happened when he let himself feel too much.

Lies.

Betrayal.

Weakness.

Disaster.

And right now, he could afford none of the above.

Seth-Aziz was depending on him. Khepesh was depending on him. The next several days could spell the difference between defeat and annihilation, or reaching his goal and savoring total victory over the enemy. And there was nothing, *nothing*, he'd allow to get in his way of knowing the sweet taste of that revenge.

Least of all a woman.

He clamped his jaw. *Especially* a woman.

Even if she did make his heart beat just a little faster.

Chapter 11

Gemma awoke alone.

The other half of the bed was empty, the tent so quiet she could hear the ghostly rasp of grains of sand bouncing off the outside walls as the winds of dawn stirred the desert to life. The room was dark. So dark she couldn't even see her toes when she wiggled them.

"Shahin?" she called softly.

Only silence echoed back at her.

In her mind, she tried to picture the inside of the tent and where the furniture and other obstacles were placed. And the position of the outer door. Sliding out of bed, she slowly inched her way toward it, bumping her knees only three or four times before hitting the stiff fabric wall with her outstretched hands. Feeling her way, she found the door and shoved aside the heavy curtain to the outside. Cool night air rushed over her face, fading starlight still lighting the oasis in a relief of moving silhouettes and shadows. Burning embers in several fire rings glowed orange and red, but no one sat around them swapping stories or dreaming. The whole camp was silent; it seemed everyone had retired to their rest.

She opened her mouth to call for Shahin again, but something kept her from releasing the sound. Closing her mouth, she listened carefully for anyone out and about. There was no one.

It would be the perfect opportunity to take a more thorough look around.

Or to escape.

Turning back inside, she scanned the dark tent interior for a candle, then ran out to the nearest fire pit to light it. Once back in the tent, she lit several others so she could see. Just in case Shahin lurked somewhere, watching her. Testing her.

But she was indeed alone.

The first thing she did was a quick search of Shahin's belongings, thinking she might find confirmation of his intentions regarding her and Josslyn. There was a desk and a sizable collection of books, but nothing relevant to the situation. No papers either. No letters, no plans. Nothing.

Was that a good thing or a bad thing?

Damn!

She should go. Now. Escape while she had the chance. Except…

Blood pumping with adrenaline, she sat on a tussock and squeezed her eyes shut. She was so torn.

On the one hand, Shahin had admitted that the cult—the *per netjer*—had plans to lure her sister permanently into their fold. And herself as well, if his statement about not letting her go in this morning was true. She wasn't so sure it was. "Collateral damage" didn't sound like she mattered one way or another. Though Shahin seemed to thoroughly enjoy her…um, company…it was Josslyn they really wanted, if his explanation last night was to be believed.

The whole situation was too bizarre for words.

And the most bizarre of all was that she hadn't already rushed out to find Bint, saddle up in a panic and set out hell-bent for leather back to the villa instead of sitting here debating with herself about what to do.

She *should* be scared out of her mind. She *should* be doubting her own sanity over all that she'd seen here. She should be horrified at her own behavior last night. Mortified at what she'd done in that bed on the other side of the tent, with a man who had turned her known world upside down and shown her things that simply weren't possible—though her eyes told her otherwise. She should be embarrassed that a virtual stranger had made her feel things she'd had no idea she was able to feel, both physically... and in her heart.

She *should* be terrified of him. Of what he did to her, inside and out. She should be running away, as fast and as far as she possibly could.

But there you go. She didn't *want* to run.

This was the chance of a lifetime! These people were *shape-shifters!* Immortals, *shemsu,* with powers beyond imagination. She wanted to stay and learn about the followers of Set-Sutekh, about their way of life and their awesome magic. She had no doubt that if she left the oasis she would never find it again, even if she wished to. Like Shangri-la, it would doubtless disappear into the sands of oblivion and the mists of time. As an ethnographer, she couldn't imagine passing up this unparalleled opportunity.

And then there was Shahin. She desperately wanted to stay with him, too. She wanted nothing more than to explore the incredible feelings he inspired in her. Experience more of them. Find new ones.

It was dangerous to stay. She knew that. Without a doubt, the most dangerous thing she would ever do in her life. But she just couldn't make herself leave.

Not yet.

Opening her eyes, she let out a long, even exhale. But there was one thing she should do. *Must* do. Soon. Before Shahin returned.

Josslyn must be warned of the danger *she* was in.

Gemma stood, went over to the antique writing desk that sat against one wall of the tent, and found a box of thick parchment stationery and a pen. She wrote Joss an urgently worded missive.

Dearest Sister,

Please don't worry. I'm fine and safe. But you must listen to me, Joss. Pack a suitcase right now and quit the villa at once. Those men from the temple ruin are coming back to kidnap you, and they must not find you there! Leave me a clue where you are, and I will join you as soon as I can. I've news of Gillian, but must hurry now to get this to you before I am discovered.

Go! Now!

And beware of the vampire! *Do not trust him.*

Love and hugs till I see you again,
Gemma

* * *

Reading it over, she underlined *Now!* three times for good measure, then folded up the note and tucked it into an envelope. But how to get it to Joss?

Searching over the contents of the tent again, her gaze stalled on a camel bag slung over the back of a chair. Making a quick decision, she grabbed it.

Hurriedly she got dressed and slipped from the tent. She'd seen approximately where the boy had taken her mare last night and she headed that way, skirting several tents, pausing whenever she heard hushed voices until she could identify where they came from and avoid meeting anyone.

She found her horse a short way along the oasis, penned in a grassy corral next to a small pond. Its youthful caregiver lay sleeping by the fence, rolled in a colorful blanket and snoring lightly.

Cautiously, she approached the corral. Bint nickered softly in greeting, and Gemma's heart raced, praying the boy wouldn't wake.

"Shh," she whispered, running her hand along the mare's mane.

The boy murmured and turned in his blanket. Gemma held her breath, her pulse leaping. But he didn't open his eyes. *Thank God.*

The night was cool, but sweat beaded on her brow as she looped the camel bag containing her note around Bint's neck, tied it securely and eased

the corral gate open, inch by slow inch. The dark
sky had already started to glow pink along the tops
of the dunes. She led the horse to just beyond the
edge of the camp that lay on the side of the coming
sunrise and the Nile Valley. The mare would find
her way home, if not by instinct, then by the smell of
the river. With any luck, before she was discovered
missing.

She gave Bint a kiss on her rough cheek and a
smack on the rear to launch her into a gallop. And
prayed her messenger would make it home.

After carefully brushing the hoof prints from the
sand with a palm frond, Gemma swiftly ran back to
Shahin's tent, got undressed and slid back into bed.
And hoped to God the man was just a shape-shifter
and not a mind reader as well.

"Where have you been?"

Shahin had been quiet when he entered, but
Gemma must have been awake and waiting for him
to return. He wondered briefly whether he should be
surprised she'd stayed in his bed rather than trying
to flee. Not that it would have done her any good.
He knew exactly where she'd have gone—the villa.
And now that they'd made love, he'd be able to get
a sense of her presence, wherever she went. He was
pleased she realized the futility of escape.

"I had some things to do," he said, unbuckling
the belt that held his scimitar.

"Josslyn?" she asked.

He could hear the worry in her voice, but he didn't want to discuss the sister with her. Down that road lay discord. "No. I am captain of the guards of Khepesh. We are on the brink of war and there is much to do."

"War?" She sat up in bed, holding the coverlet over her breasts. He didn't like that. He wanted to see her.

His body stirred as he walked toward her shedding his clothes. "With Haru-Re, the high priest of the Sun God Re-Horakhti," he explained, "and his followers." He got into bed and gathered her in his arms, pulling her down on top of him.

"But that's terrible," she said, her voice even more worried. She didn't resist him, but she didn't drop the conversation either. "Why war?"

"It is a long-standing battle," he said impatiently, driving his fingers through her hair and bringing her mouth to his. "Forget it. We have far pleasanter things than war to think about at the moment."

After a few seconds' hesitation, he felt her tension ease. "Such as?" she asked coyly.

He fisted his cock and fitted it to her as he urged her to straddle him. It was a rare day he let a woman dominate him, but for some reason it didn't feel that way with Gemma.

"This," he said, and whispered a command into her mouth. Graphic. Unambiguous. Forceful.

Her body shivered and she softly moaned his name. His heart hitched at the breathless sound of it on her lips. The emotion it contained sounded so honest and true. But it wasn't. It couldn't be.

He was in complete control as he thrust up into her, eliciting a groan of pleasure from deep in her throat.

It was the first of many.

When he was finished with her, they were both slick from exertion and panting with blissful completion. She collapsed in a heap across his chest.

"Keep doing this," she said on a half moan, half sigh, "and making me stay with you here won't be a problem. It'll be impossible to get me to leave."

He smiled. "Good." He wrapped his arms around her and prepared to grab a short catnap before taking off for his morning task. "I'm glad we're in complete agreement."

But he never got the chance for sleep. A loud call and an insistent scratching sounded at the outside door. Alarm coursed through his mind as he rolled out of bed, grabbing his trousers. No one would dare disturb him this morning unless it was an urgent matter.

"What?" he barked, shoving aside the curtained

tent flap. He was surprised to see Hasim standing there, hopping from one foot to the other.

"My lord! She is gone!" the boy cried.

Shahin frowned. He knew very well Gemma was *not* gone. "Who?"

"Madam's mare," Hasim burst out, the explanation rushing from his mouth like a sandstorm. "The horse is nowhere to be found! It's all my fault! I'm sorry, my lord! She must have gotten loose last night. I swear I didn't mean to fall asleep—"

Shahin held up his hand and the verbal torrent ceased abruptly. "You've searched for the mare?"

"Yes! Everywhere, sir!"

This was not good. "Tracks?"

"They are going toward the east."

Home to the villa. He cursed. "Summon a few of the men. We must try and intercept the animal before it reaches Josslyn Haliday."

The boy dashed off and Shahin ducked back into his tent, waving a hand to light a couple of the sconce torches. He could easily see in the dark, but he wanted Gemma to be able to see him when he questioned her.

But she looked so temptingly disheveled, so drowsily content curled up naked in the center of his bed, that his tongue could not bring itself to break the harmony between them with the accusations echoing in his mind. Maybe he was wrong. Maybe she had nothing to do with this.

"Leaving again?" she asked sleepily when he began to dress.

"Yes. Go back to sleep," he told her with a kiss.

In less than three minutes he'd readied himself and strode outside to meet his men. The last thing he did was to throw a spell of containment over the tent to prevent her from leaving. She might appear innocent, but he was no fool. Then he and his men shifted and flew like the wind to the villa.

But it was too late.

When they arrived, the missing horse was in the stable, contentedly munching on straw.

And Josslyn Haliday had already fled.

A thorough search of the villa revealed only one clue. But it was enough. On the floor next to the sofa lay a familiar camel bag. Shahin's *own* camel bag.

There was just one explanation possible for its presence here. *Gemma*.

Fury surged through his veins. For this, she would pay, and pay dearly.

Chapter 12

Nephtys was not terribly surprised when Shahin returned to Khepesh in a rage several hours after he'd left and reported that Josslyn Haliday had taken flight before he could capture her. He was a seething mass of anger, blaming it on the sister he'd taken to his camp. She, apparently, had found a way to warn Josslyn what was about to befall her.

One thing you had to give the Haliday sisters: They were not stupid. Nor were they inclined to lie back passively and accept a fate they didn't agree with. Nephtys admired them for their bravery.

Despite its complete futility.

For in the end, they were as powerless to fight

their appointed destiny as she herself. The only question was, what that ultimate destiny would be. She wished she would have a vision that made it clear which sister was supposed to belong to Seth-Aziz. It would make certain decisions so much easier.

Seth and Shahin were gazing expectantly at her now, as if she had all the answers.

"You must find Josslyn," she told Lord Shahin. There was no question of letting the last sister remain free, regardless of her final disposition. "We cannot take any chances. Our situation is too precarious at the moment. If we don't run her to ground, you can be sure Haru-Re will, once he gets wind of her."

Seth paced slowly back and forth, following the line of columns rimming the wall of the audience chamber. He was visibly tired, his skin growing translucent, his beautiful body soft with fatigue. He needed blood, and soon.

"Where would she have gone?" he asked Shahin. "Will she try to get out of Egypt?"

"I doubt it," the captain of the guard ground out. "I've been assured she won't leave her sisters behind, especially if she thinks they are in danger."

Nephtys respected family loyalty, but it would not make Shahin's job any easier. "You must use all your powers on Gemma and find out where Josslyn could be hiding," she urged.

Shahin glowered. "If Gemma knows, you can be sure I'll get it out of her."

"Go, then," Seth said. "Send word when you know something."

"Likewise," Shahin returned, and looked at Nephtys. "It would be very useful if you could call forth a vision to help locate the woman."

She nodded and lied. "I shall try."

Not a chance. She would not seek a vision if there was any possibility that Haru-Re would appear in it again. Which he would. The man was proving viciously relentless.

But the sheikh didn't know that. With a graceful bow to her brother, he strode out of the chamber, a determined scowl firmly in place. Nephtys felt briefly sorry for his captive. Whatever bliss Gemma Haliday had experienced in his bed last night was about to be shattered by her lover's wrath. Obviously, there was no way the unlucky woman could know that betraying this man's trust was the very worst thing she could have done, but she would suffer for her actions nonetheless.

"Are you going to tell me about it?" Seth asked calmly, jerking Nephtys's attention back to him.

She blinked and stilled, her mind racing like a gazelle through the possibilities of what he might be referring to.

"About what?" she asked, striving for composure.

She did not want her brother to know about the dream-visions. But even in his weakening state, his intuition was still sharp and flawless, and she had been thinking of them almost nonstop. He must have sensed it.

He closed his eyes, as though conserving energy. "You've been seeing him, haven't you." Not a question, but an accusation filled with tightly bound wrath.

Nevertheless she attempted innocence. "Who?"

"You know very well who I mean!" The ire flooded out. He opened his eyes and pinned her with a piercing glare. The room swirled with his dark power. "I'd say it was in a vision, but it's more than that. You've seen him in the flesh. You've *been* with him," Seth bit out. *"Haven't you?"* he demanded.

Her jaw dropped in consternation. "How did you…"

Seth turned on her, his gaze furious as he jabbed the air with a finger to emphasize every point. She felt the aura of each jab punch into her chest. "You've been covering your neck with scarves and collars for the past week. You reek of vampire magic. And you just lied to Shahin about seeking a vision." He advanced on her, his weary eyes narrowed to slits. "Do I not have enough to contend with without my own sister consorting with the enemy behind my back?" Seth rarely raised his voice, but he almost shouted the last.

She stood her ground, but it wasn't easy facing down an incensed demigod. Haru-Re was not the only one who could crush her like a scarab beetle. In his present state, Seth might do it accidentally... or on purpose.

She held up her palms in supplication. "*Hadu*, that is exactly why I didn't tell you. With everything going on, I wanted to try and deal with this hateful intrusion on my own."

He made a visible effort to calm himself.

"And how's that going for you?" he snapped, as though the answer weren't obvious.

"Not all that well," she admitted, knowing the truth was the only viable option at this point. "Haru-Re has found a way to transmigrate physically, through my dreams."

Seth looked stunned, suddenly wide awake. "He can make himself appear? Here? In Khepesh?"

She nodded miserably. "He claims he's able to do it using an ancient, forgotten spell he found in his library."

Seth's face went stony. "It's difficult to believe such a spell could ever have been lost."

"I agree." She let out a long sigh and took a few steps away from him. She couldn't think within the field of angry power still rolling off him in waves.

"Although I suppose it's possible it was a carefully guarded secret belonging to a conquered *per netjer*. He's taken over many smaller ones through the years. And like you, he always spares their libraries and adds the scrolls to his own collection. It's possible the spell has languished and only now been rediscovered."

She was hoping Seth would be distracted by the speculation, but she should have known better.

"What exactly has he done to you?" he demanded. "What sedition has he asked you to perform for him?"

It hurt her pride a little that her brother believed Ray would have no other purpose for his nocturnal visits than treachery. Not that Seth was wrong...no matter how much she wanted to think otherwise.

She swallowed and wandered over to the dual thrones where Seth sat during his audiences as high priest before his people. Over the centuries, a handful of consorts had occupied the smaller of the two; sometimes at his request, she herself had sat in it as his trusted adviser. She ran her fingers along the cool silver arm of the throne, not daring to sit in it now.

"He wants me to abandon you and go back to him," she answered bitterly. "But that is hardly news. We both know why he wants me, and it's not because of his undying love for his former slave girl."

Seth let out a breath and his face softened a fraction. "Thank beneficent Ptah for that. Otherwise, I fear I would have lost you long ago."

She started to say "Never!" but didn't. There was no use denying the all-too-real possibility. Having stayed in love with the bastard for so long, who was to say but her incalculable weakness might in the end win out, even over her strong and inviolable family loyalty? An ugly truth that shamed her as nothing else could.

Understanding her dismay over her inner failing, Seth opened his arms to her. She went into them gratefully. "I've been trying to stay awake, spending every moment I can in our library, hoping to find a counter-spell or a ward against it."

"And?"

"Nothing yet."

He grunted, and before she realized what he was doing, he unfastened her jeweled collar and slid it from around her neck, exposing the fading marks of the first vampire bite Ray had given her a week ago. Seth gently tipped her head to one side to examine it, murder glittering in his eyes as brightly as the collar. He knew better than to touch the marks. Or even breathe on them.

At length, he asked, "Are there more?"

She lowered her gaze. He knew their adversary well. "Yes," she admitted.

He didn't ask where. "So he fucks you."

Her face went hot. "Yes." Because that was the word for it. Ray was not a man who made love.

"Whore-son of a jackal," Seth ground out. "Would it help if someone stayed with you in your room as you sleep and kept guard?"

"I don't think so." She shook her head. "I don't know how to explain it. He's not…there with me, in the place where I fall asleep. It's like he's in my head, except—" she raised her fingers to hover over the bite "—our bodies are real. *This* is real."

Seth didn't often appear worried, but now a shadow of concern moved across his already-drawn face. "A very powerful spell. Luckily, it must only work with those he has a positive emotional connection with. Otherwise, by now he would surely have come into my dreams and tried to kill me."

She gasped. She hadn't thought of that. Then she frowned. "A love spell? You think?" Though she wasn't so sure about the positive emotional part. But if that was true, it could narrow down prospective sources of the spell. Not all gods could use emotions for their magic.

Seth released her and went over to drop down onto the larger throne. He leaned back and steepled his fingers thoughtfully. "A love spell makes sense and answers the question of why he hasn't come after me in my dreams. But I don't like it. I don't like that he has such power over you."

"You think *I* do?" she cried. "I haven't had more than a few hours' sleep in the past week. I'm desperate to end this torture!"

Seth tilted his head. "He doesn't pleasure you?"

"Yes! Yes, of course he does." She put her hands to her temples and squeezed her eyes shut. "That's why I'm so worried. You know the sensual power a vampire has over a woman, even a priestess of my magical abilities. I'm terrified he'll make me do something I don't want to do, just to feel that incredible pleasure again. It's an unholy addiction. I'm so afraid I'll break."

"That would not be a good thing."

"No, it wouldn't." She felt the hot press of tears sting her eyes. "I need to find a way to defeat that spell. *Soon.* Or it may just be me who's the downfall of all of Khepesh."

Shahin stalked across the oasis toward his tent. With every step he took, the ground quaked and rolled, his element agitated beyond rational control. Along the way, he paused only long enough to toss his scabbard and scimitar to one of his men. He did not want to be armed when he confronted Gemma.

She was reclining among the pillows under the front canopy of his tent, a Turkish coffeepot and demitasse sitting on the low brass table at her elbow, a book in her hand. He'd had one of the women take away her ugly riding clothes this morning, and had conjured a cupboardful of beautiful dresses for her instead. She'd chosen one in emerald green, a thin, flowing concoction of silk that fluttered about her shapely calves in the morning breeze. Her feet were bare. At any other time, the sight of her would have caused his body to quicken with possessiveness.

Now he wondered what evil demon had seized hold of his wits to have him bring her here. The woman was a curse he did not need.

She watched his approach uncertainly, her smile of greeting fading from her face.

"You're upset," she said, grabbing the cup and saucer as the ground roiled under them.

What was her first clue?

"Josslyn has disappeared," he told her, to gauge her reaction.

"Oh?" The single word contained guilt and no surprise.

He growled an oath. "This was *your* doing. *Wasn't it?*" Furious, he closed the distance between them. The tent shook just as furiously as the earthquakes spilled from his anger.

The book flew from her hand as she comprehended

his rage. She scuttled backward on the pillows. "I d-don't know w-what you're talking about."

He threw the camel bag at her feet, then swooped down and grasped her shoulders in a hard grip, hauling her up to stand. "By the blood of Sekhmet, *do not lie to me!*"

Her body trembled, but her eyes held more than a shade of defiance. "All right. I did it! I let Bint loose to warn Josslyn." To his disbelief, her gaze melted a little and she touched his chest with her fingers, almost in a caress. A temblor purred through the sand beneath her. "Shahin, I am here with you now of my own desire, but surely you didn't think I'd let you kidnap my sister without a fight? She deserves a choice in whether to join the *per netjer*, and certainly in whether to marry a stranger—a stranger who's a vampire!"

The memory of his own sister's forced "union" skated through Shahin's mind, tempering his anger at this woman's betrayal as nothing else could have. Tempered, but not diminished. He reined in the fury of his element and pushed her toward the tent door. "Get. Inside."

Now she did look worried. "No!"

She tried to dig in her heels, but he was in no mood. He lifted her, threw her over his shoulder and carried her in. She screamed and beat his back with her fists. He barely felt it. No one in camp paid the slightest attention to her cries.

"Stop," he ordered.

He set her on her feet, grabbing her wrist when she would shrink away from him. A few of the torch sconces still burned, casting the room into a chiaroscuro of dancing light and shadow. He could smell her sudden acrid fear, hear the cacophony of her out-of-control heartbeat. She was under his complete power and they both knew it.

"What are you going to do to me?" she asked hoarsely.

"I haven't decided," he growled. "I should just kill you and save myself dealing with your treachery. If Kilpatrick had done that with your sister, Khepesh would not now be facing annihilation, and I would not have failed in my duty to the god!"

Her eyes rounded and she swallowed. "You can't mean that. You wouldn't kill a woman you made love to all night. You couldn't."

"Made *love?*" He gave a snort of derision to show what he thought of that concept. "I used your body, nothing more."

He ignored the spike of remorse he felt when her lips parted a fraction and her face went carefully neutral. But he could see in her eyes he'd hurt her, which was complete insanity, because to be hurt, she had to feel something for him.

Or think she did. Was that infernal spell *still* working?

"I see," she murmured, casting her wounded eyes downward.

"Lest you carry any illusions, you are here to share my bed for a short while, nothing more. Do not deceive yourself that this fantasy of yours involves any deeper feelings from either of us. Or that I am interested in any kind of permanence."

"I see," she repeated.

"I am easily bored."

She just looked at the floor.

He paced away from her, refusing to feel an iota of guilt. This was all *her* doing. Even so, the earthquakes stilled.

He turned. "Now, tell me where Josslyn has gone," he commanded her.

"I don't know," she said. Her chin lifted stubbornly and her gaze met his. "And guess what? I wouldn't tell you even if I *did* know."

He regarded her, suddenly feeling absolutely calm. "Oh, you would tell me," he assured. He took a step toward her. "You *will* tell me."

Her chin went higher. "What are you going to do, torture me?"

"Have a care," he quietly cautioned. Though it wouldn't be the kind of torture she expected. Not by any measure. "You forget who I am. *What* I am."

"You are Sheikh Shahin, legendary leader of the death warriors." She leaned toward him and pressed a finger into his chest. "Well, Sheikh Shahin, do your worst. You may have me in your power, but I'll be *damned* if I let you have my sister, too."

His lips curved sinisterly. She had no idea what she was toying with here. He could break her without lifting a finger. Have anything he wanted from her with a mere thought.

In minutes.

Seconds.

But no, he decided. It would be much more amusing to take his time teaching her a lesson.

In the end, he would get what he wanted. Along with the greater gratification of her obedience.

Chapter 13

Gemma did her best not to be terrified out of her wits. She'd never seen Shahin this angry before. He'd leashed the earthquakes, but his otherworldly energy swirled in the air around him, so thick and heavy you could almost touch it.

But she knew he wouldn't hurt her. He *wouldn't*. After the night they'd had together, she refused to believe it of him.

Even though her mind screamed at her *Shrink back! Escape!* she stepped closer to him. And closer still. Until she stood right in front of him, her body brushing against his.

He might deny he had feelings for her, but she

knew better. She knew exactly what kind of feelings he had for her.

His eyes narrowed to black slits. But trust was not among those sentiments.

Why?

He was like a different person from last night. One who didn't even see her. She wondered what had happened in his past to make the man so hard and cold on the outside. She knew very well he wasn't that way on the inside. She'd had ample proof of it last night.

"Shahin," she said, striving to sound far calmer than she felt. "You don't want to do this."

"But I do," he refuted, and reached for her.

At the touch of his hands, his magical energy crept up her arms like a bath of warm fur. It melted over her, higher and lower, enveloping her whole body, taking control of her, robbing her of her strength. She shivered. Loving how it felt…knowing she shouldn't let herself succumb to it. Such a show of domination, of supernatural "otherness" should frighten her. But it just felt…good.

She couldn't help herself, she put her arms around him. He stiffened. "Just how will you torture me?" she asked seductively.

He was silent for several heartbeats. At length, he said, "You are either a very brave or a very foolish woman, Gemma Haliday."

He wasn't the first person to tell her that. Mostly it had been a comment on her returning again and again to Egypt to do her ethnographical fieldwork. But just as her love for this country was too complicated to explain, so were her feelings for this man. He'd hurt her just now, denying their connection so brutally. But she didn't believe him. Perhaps bravely, perhaps foolishly, she trusted Egypt to keep her safe. And she trusted Shahin as well.

She looked up at him and felt herself drowning in the press of his overwhelming power. It was like sinking underwater, except she could breathe. Sort of.

He mirrored her gaze evenly. "I could bespell you," he said, "and you would tell me everything you know."

"Which is nothing," she returned. "How could I? I've been here with you for two days."

"But you know your sister," he pointed out. "I could shower you with pain, and you would beg to tell me where she is so that it would stop."

"You wouldn't do that," she said without hesitation. "You're not that cruel."

He stared at her for a long moment. "I could touch you," he said, his voice going low and suggestive, "and you would beg to tell me where she is to make me continue."

"You'll do that anyway," she murmured, and

brushed her lips over his. "And believe me, it's not torture."

He closed his eyes for a split second, then opened them again fiercely. "You are a witch," he gritted out, stepped into her and covered her lips with his. Erotic energy spilled through her, like he was feeding it to her with his tongue.

"And you are a demon," she returned. For that was exactly what he was, an ancient warrior come from the realm of the underworld to claim her soul for his own purposes. And with growing desperation she realized a terrible truth. She would give it to him, gladly, if only he wanted to claim her heart as well. She shuddered with need and kissed him back, swallowing the magical essence of him, eating at his mouth and his lips, wanting more of it. Of him.

He kissed her until they were both shaking and panting with want. And then he pulled away with a low growl. He held her body apart from his with fingers like steel talons in the flesh of her arms. He glared down at her as if what he really wanted to do was cast her away from himself forever.

"Please, Shahin," she whispered. Not really knowing what she expected of him, not as a leader of the *per netjer*, nor as her lover, but having the sinking feeling she would never get what she needed to feel okay with any of this, on any level. "I honestly don't know where Josslyn has gone."

Whether he believed her, there was no way of telling. Within the storm cloud of his face, his eyes were like black voids, the gold rings around his pupils flashing like lightning. "I'll make a bargain with you," he said, his deep voice vibrating with something she dared not guess.

Speak of the devil… "What kind of bargain?" she asked, licking her lips, gathering a taste of him on her tongue. Weakening further.

"Come with me to Khepesh. Meet the man intended for your sister. See for yourself that he is a worthy match for her."

Whatever bargain she'd expected, this wasn't it. She gaped at him. "You want to take me to your temple-palace?" She didn't know whether to be thrilled or scared stiff.

"The *per netjer*, yes. Meet Seth-Aziz. See how we live. Make up your own mind if your sister could be happy with him."

"That's not for me to decide," she argued. She tried to pull away, but he wouldn't let her go. "And what if I don't like him? What happens then?"

"Even the Lady Gillian found Seth-Aziz to be a good man," he reasoned. "She liked and respected him."

"And yet she ran away with another. Betrayed him, rather than marry him."

The lightning in Shahin's eyes flashed brighter.

"Because of Lord Kilpatrick, not Seth-Aziz, or what he is."

A shiver went down her spine at the thought of being married to a vampire…feeding a vampire with blood from your own veins…having sex with a vampire. This wasn't some silly teen movie where everything was Hollywood-perfect, where no one got hurt and it never got ugly. This was the real thing, bloody and messy.

"Are you sure about that?" she asked, totally unconvinced.

He leveled her a scorching gaze and let her go. He turned and strode toward the door. "I won't force you, Gemma. You must enter Khepesh of your own free will."

His power still roiled like a living thing around her. She knew he could compel her to do anything he wanted easily enough. So why didn't he?

He lifted the curtained door and held it open for her, silently commanding her to go with him.

Did she really have a choice? Besides, maybe she'd feel better about all this if she met the man ultimately responsible for drawing her and her sisters onto this fateful, otherworldly path.

Or maybe she wouldn't. In which case, she'd decide then what to do about it.

She followed Shahin outside and watched nervously as he sent Hasim to fetch his men, then he sketched a small design in the air with his fingers and murmured an incantation.

Several large shapes began to materialize from a swirling mist in front of them. *The ghost camels.* One of the apparitions trotted over to Shahin and lowered itself onto its belly for him. He beckoned to her to come.

Warily, she went to him. He gathered her body in his arms and seemingly effortlessly mounted the huge beast and settled her on the soft saddle in front of him. With a chorus of masculine shouts and animal hisses, his men also mounted and joined them. As one, the troop of warriors took off, loping up the dunes and galloping forth across the desert sands. Toward what…only God knew.

Shahin held her tight against his chest and wrapped his *bisht* around them both as a shield against the hot wind and blazing sun.

It was only then she had a chance to really think about what she was doing. And that's when the fear began to climb within her.

Sheikh Shahin, the legendary harbinger of death, was taking her to Khepesh, *per netjer* of Set-Sutekh, the God of Darkness and Chaos, dwelling place of his immortal followers. To meet the vampire demigod Seth-Aziz.

But Shahin had never said anything about leaving

again. What if the cult had other plans for her? What if once inside their lair, they wouldn't let her go?

He had just told her she would only share his bed for a short while. What would happen to her after he tired of her?

What if that pomegranate martini really *had* been the updated version of the old myth and she had eaten the six seeds that doomed her to live in Set-Sutekh's underworld palace forever, once Shahin ceased to be amused by her?

She turned in his arms, striving to mask the rush of panic that crept through her bones. She caught his gaze with hers. "You aren't going to leave me there without you, are you?" she asked. "At Khepesh?"

He didn't look away, but he didn't answer either.

Suddenly a bolt of raw terror stabbed through her. *"Shahin?"* Her heart stalled completely. Yes, she'd angered him by defying his wishes, but..." You wouldn't do that, would you?"

His mouth thinned and he regarded her for a long, tense moment. "I haven't decided," was all he said.

Shahin knew he was losing his mind.

He must be. Because most definitely the organ he was thinking with at the moment did *not* reside in his head.

He watched Gemma's face drain of color and

actually felt a stab of guilt over his unfeeling words, both now and earlier.

By the rod of Osiris!

He turned aside and ignored her. Or tried to. Even though it wasn't easy with the warmth of her body pressed intimately against his, and the weight of her uncertain gaze upon him.

He'd promised Seth to use all his powers to find Josslyn Haliday. A simple spell of veracity would make Gemma spill her secrets, including where her sister had fled, if she knew. But Shahin had not cast the spell. Why? Because he couldn't bear the thought of seeing that trusting, adoring look in her eyes turn to suspicion, or worse, hatred, when she realized what he had done.

Gemma was like no other woman he'd ever met. She wasn't afraid of him. She didn't want anything from him. Not money or gifts. Not magic. Not eternal life. She hadn't asked him for a single thing. Well, all right she had, in bed. But those things he'd been more than happy to grant her.

What he *wasn't* happy to gift her with was any part of his heart, or any of his emotions at all. And yet, inexplicably, he found himself doing just that.

He yearned to let go and allow himself to feel something for this woman who was so unique, as his reckless heart was urging him to do.

Had he not learned his lesson the first time a

woman had used her wiles on him? Had he and his family not suffered enough for that misplaced trust?

Nephtys had tried to convince him not all women were like the lover who'd betrayed him so long ago. But in his position, how could he take that chance? As captain of the guard, he could not afford a mistake that might jeopardize the lives of all those who depended upon him for their safety. If his emotions were compromised, he could not trust his decisions.

And he'd be an utter fool to trust Gemma Haliday.

He really *should* leave her at Khepesh. Remove the temptation of her from his life altogether. That was where she was destined to end up anyway. What was wrong with hastening along the inevitable?

Unfortunately, he knew exactly what was wrong with it.

He wanted her right where she was.

In his arms. Warm. Pliable. Giving. Loving.

Even if it was just a fantasy illusion.

They reached the *gebel* entrance to the palace, and he waved it open. Without breaking stride, the camels plunged down into the Realm of Darkness.

Gemma clung to him. He held her as they rode deeper and deeper, down into the very heart of the underworld. Until a faint light pierced the dark, growing into the brilliant glow of a hundred torches.

They'd reached their destination.

The Great Western Gate of Khepesh.

The camels snorted and brayed, turning sideways and shying from the burning torches as the men reined them in.

Gemma sat awestruck, unable to move as she gazed up at the monumental silver gate before her.

Soaring at least three stories above them, the portal was really a huge double door. It seemed to be made of solid, glittering silver and was flanked by tall, lotus-shaped, fire-burning torches. Both wings of the door were engraved with row upon row of intricately wrought hieroglyphics. The cartouche of Set-Sutekh graced the center of each, along with a reverse *wedget*, the left eye of Horus—the symbol of Set-Sutekh's victory over the Sun God.

She still hadn't quite believed that Shahin was bringing her to the mythical dwelling place of the God of the Moon. But she was starting to be convinced.

"My God," Gemma whispered threadily, clutching Shahin's hand with trembling fingers. "It's magnificent."

"Just wait," he said. He lifted her off the camel and they approached the gate.

It made a long, deep clang and slowly started

to open. The air around them vibrated, conveying something far deeper than sound. It was as though the power and magic of the tomb-palace could not be contained by mere walls. She felt the energy rise around her, electric and potent, more and more with every inch the gate opened. A shiver sifted down her arms, raising a rash of goose flesh.

She eased behind Shahin's body, totally spooked.

He urged her forward again. "Don't be afraid. No one's going to hurt you."

This coming from the man who had just threatened to torture her.

Inside the gate, a crowd of people was gathering. They looked…interesting. Some were dressed in modern clothes, some in the ancient Egyptian style and others in every imaginable fashion in between.

"Why are they dressed so differently?" she whispered to Shahin, focusing on the trivial details so she wouldn't have to think about the big picture of what was happening.

He glanced down at her, then back at the crowd, as though he'd never noticed before. "We were all born in different times. I suppose we wear what we're most comfortable in. There are no rules."

Fascinating.

She suddenly noticed a tall, stern-looking man

standing in the middle of the crowd. He had on splendid robes of shining black with a sash of crimson spanning his trim waist. Most of the people were peering out at her with curiosity, but this man had a distinct frown on his handsome face.

Omigod. It must be him. *The vampire.*

"My lord," Shahin said with a formal bow, confirming her guess. He touched her shoulder and she found herself going down on her knees under a power other than her own. "You must kneel before your lord and master, Seth-Aziz, Guardian of Darkness and high priest to Set-Sutekh, Lord of the Night Sky."

She wasn't sure what protocol demanded when meeting a demigod, but she took a stab at it, inclining her head nervously. "It's an honor to meet you. I'm Gemma Haliday."

His eyes narrowed and he glanced at a woman standing next to him. She had flame-red hair and a youthful, kind face. She gave her head a small shake. He didn't look pleased, but he turned back and spoke to Shahin. "Does this woman come willingly?"

"Yes, my lord. She is willing."

Wait. Willing to do what?

Shahin strode through the gate, leaving her on her knees and on her own.

"Very well." Seth-Aziz raised his hands to her, palms up, and said in a voice loud enough for all to hear, "If you would join us, Gemma Haliday, and become one of the *shemsu*, the immortal followers of Set-Sutekh, rise now and walk through the portal."

She blinked.

Hold on.

Join us? Become *immortal?* Shahin hadn't said anything about any of *that*. She freely admitted to a healthy professional curiosity about Khepesh, as well as being personally intrigued by the possibilities and implications of its existence and what it could mean for her. But join? Before she knew what she was getting herself into? And for how long...?

And wasn't he being just a *load* of help now, returning a blank stare to her anxious gaze? Why was he acting so damn aloof? Was he still mad at her for warning Joss? Or had he tired of her in his bed already and simply lured her here to be rid of her?

She pressed her lips together.

Well, screw him.

And screw this whole ridiculous situation. Enough was enough.

She got to her feet, formed her lips into a cordial smile for the high priest and announced, "I don't. Freaking. *Think* so."

Then she took a deep breath, spun on a heel and started to run.

Chapter 14

Shahin stared impassively after the woman and muttered an oath.

Beside him, he heard Seth-Aziz sigh. "Well, so much for willing."

"She panicked. She just needs a little more convincing, my lord," Shahin said.

Seth grunted. "Sekhmet's teeth, what *is* it about these accursed Haliday women that makes them so damned defiant?"

Nephtys frowned. "Can't she see this is for her own good? Does she *want* to be turned into a *shabti* and spend the rest of eternity as a servant with no mind of her own?"

"I haven't actually told her about that part yet," Shahin confessed. "I'd hoped to avoid threats."

Seth rolled his eyes. "And how's *that* working for you?"

It was Shahin's turn to sigh. "Not terribly well."

The crowd around them stirred and started murmuring curiously, wondering what would happen next. But no one left.

"You should fetch her back before she gets too lost," Nephtys urged.

"Yes," Shahin said but he didn't move.

"Any luck finding Josslyn?" Seth asked.

"Not yet. As you see, Gemma is being very stubborn. I suggested this meeting with you to convince her that her sister would like you."

Seth's brows shot up. "A unique approach."

"It was worth a shot. I guess I forgot to mention she must be willing to become one of the *shemsu* to enter Khepesh."

"Another small detail, admittedly," Seth said sardonically.

Shahin considered. "Perhaps a bribe is in order."

"I thought you'd already offered her your body," Nephtys muttered.

Shahin made a face at her. "My lady is very amusing, indeed. No, I was thinking of her mother.

Before she fled, Gillian discovered evidence in the library that Haru-Re took their mother captive twenty years ago. The family has thought all these years that Isobelle Haliday is dead, but I would be willing to bet she is still alive."

"And no doubt living at Petru as a *shabti*," Nephtys reminded him. "I don't know that finding out one's mother has been kidnapped and robbed of her personality is exactly the best way to endear Gemma to life as an immortal."

Shahin winced inwardly. For three-hundred years he had insisted to himself and anyone else who brought up the subject that his family was lost to him forever, and the best way to deal with his horrendous loss was to forget them completely.

It hadn't worked. He would never forget them or their fates. Never.

"Perhaps," he conceded. "But when all is said and done, I'd rather my own sister were still alive, even if living her life as a *shabti*. I still have hope of meeting my mother again, though I know she will not recognize her only son. But just seeing her would ease my heart."

Nephtys met his gaze sympathetically. "You're right, of course. Anything is better than never seeing your loved ones again."

Seth shot her a sharp glance, held it for a millisecond, then turned to him. "Go to your woman, Shahin. Talk some sense into her. But I grow impatient. I'll expect word from you before nightfall."

Shahin inclined his head. "I am your humble servant, my lord."

Then he strode out to find Gemma and stop her from sealing herself into an unhappy fate that would please no one.

Least of all himself.

It didn't take Shahin long to locate Gemma. She had gotten completely turned around in the pitch blackness of the access tunnels, as he'd known she would, and had doubled back on herself. One must be an initiate of the Guardian of Secrets and Darkness to find one's way through the stygian labyrinth of the hidden desert entrance to Khepesh Palace.

He heard her muttering from yards away.

"I swear to God, I will *never* do anything impetuous ever again. And just freaking *shoot* me if I ever look at another tall, dark, handsome stranger."

Despite everything, he felt himself smile and halted, letting her rant.

"This is *so* not happening. I am just having one long, very weird nightma—"

Suddenly her grumbling stopped in mid-word

and he heard her suck in a breath. The air around him shivered.

There was another curse. Then, "There's no use hiding from me, Shahin," she ground out. "I can feel you lurking out there."

Again, waves of shivers came from her, rolling over his skin with a tingling sensation, which was strange. He'd never had a mortal's energy reach out to him before.

He waved a hand and a wall torch sprang to life. Gemma stood in the middle of the tunnel rubbing her hands up and down her arms. She took an involuntary step backward.

"I'm not going back there," she said curtly, her spine going pike straight. "You said I must go to Khepesh of my own free will, but not that I would have to join the cult to do so."

He tipped his head at her. "What did you think it meant?" he asked, feeling an edge of impatience. "Did you really think that after you entered the secret gateway of the palace we could ever let you go again? You *must* join us, *kalila*. Or..."

"Or what?"

He pressed his lips together. "You would not like the alternative."

"And what is that?"

His irritation got the better of him. "To become a *shabti*," he bit out.

She looked taken aback. "One of those blue faience figurines they find by the thousands in ancient Egyptian tombs?"

"In essence," he affirmed, "except alive. A *shabti* is a person who has been robbed of his or her will and individual personality, and exists but to serve his or her master. In this case, Seth-Aziz."

It was like he had physically struck her. "That's horrible! You *do* that to people?"

He shook his head. "Not at Khepesh. Not anymore, other than as a very last resort, if there is no other way to ensure the safety of our people. We would far rather have someone who has learned our secrets become one of the *shemsu*, a valuable member of our community. We abhor the practice of slaves."

"But if I refuse to join of my own free will, that's what will happen?"

He wasn't going to lie, and anyway, it was best she knew the truth. "Yes," he said. Perhaps knowing the consequence of refusal would finally bring her into line.

Naturally, it didn't.

Anger washed across her face. "Nice of you to tell me *before* I learned your secrets."

"It wouldn't have mattered. I've explained all of this. We are your destiny, Gemma, one way or the other. I'd hoped you wouldn't see it as a bad fate.

That you might choose to…to be with me, all on your own."

The words were out before he could stop them. By the cock of Min! *Be* with him? Had he lost his mind?

Luckily, she thought so, too. "Be with you? For how long?"

"As long as I wish to keep you," he snapped.

Her face told what she thought of that. But she tried logic rather than emotion.

"Regardless, you can't expect me to abandon my life in America. I have friends, a job, responsibilities. I can't just disappear and leave them."

"You can and you will. Of course you'll have to write letters, explaining that you've decided to remain in Egypt." He schooled his impatience and took a step toward her, driven by some urge he didn't understand. "You could say you've met a man and fallen in love and he asked you to stay."

She stared at him, her eyes suddenly shuttered by wary uncertainty. "Are you?" she blurted out. "Asking me to stay?"

He came partially to his senses and took another step toward her. "Have *you?* Fallen in love?"

She licked her lips. He felt another tingle wash across his skin. "Don't be ridiculous. I barely know you, Shahin."

She was lying, which explained why his harsh

words had hurt her earlier. The trouble was, he didn't know if he really meant them. Bored? He couldn't ever imagine being bored by this woman.

And that scared the hell out of him. How could this have happened to either of them so quickly?

"That's not an answer," he said.

"It's the only one you're getting," she said and turned to walk away.

He closed the distance between them, spun her around and slapped his hands on the wall to either side of her shoulders, trapping her. "You don't seem to understand. *Life as you knew it before is over.* I'm trying to make this transition as easy for you as I can, offering you something else instead. Something we can both enjoy, together."

"What about *my* wishes? And the wishes of my sister?"

"It was *you* who sought *me* out, Gemma," he reminded her tersely. "As for your sister, that was not my decision."

She glared at him. "Just following orders?"

"Not about you." And wasn't that the truth. He gripped her chin and kissed her. Hard. She resisted at first but couldn't hold out against the power of their attraction. She melted into him.

He wrapped his arms around her and broke the kiss. "I want you with me, Gemma." For the long or short term, it didn't matter. All that mattered now was that he possessed her. "I'll do my best to make you happy."

He felt her fingers curl into his *bisht*. "But only if I join your cult."

Mithra's *balls* she was stubborn!

"We are *not* a cult," he ground out. "Yes, we serve Set-Sutekh but not as fanatics. You can keep your convictions if you but serve him, too."

"How can you expect me to be happy spending eternity serving a god I don't believe in?" she argued.

He could see her inner struggle, but it was so unnecessary.

"Don't you?" he asked. "Do you not believe in the darkness of the night sky and the strength of the wind in your face, and the truth that chaos rules the world? Even your Western mathematicians bow to the Lord of Chaos with their theories of the universe."

"Not exactly," she said, objecting to his characterization.

"*Yes,* exactly," he persuaded. "We don't worship Set-Sutekh as an idol or even as a being, but we revere him as a symbol for the aspects of the world over which he rules. I told you, I am a Christian and I believe in one God. But I also believe there are many facets to that God and the limitless universe of His Creation. We at Khepesh serve one small part of the Unknowable Whole, that's all."

She shook her head. "But wind, darkness and chaos? Even if I completely understood what you are saying, I would not choose to serve those aspects."

He smiled and let her slip away from his embrace. "Without darkness there is no light. Without chaos, no order. They are two halves of one coin, *kalila*. To honor the one half is to honor the other equally, and to be in awe of the amazing rightness of God's Great Plan."

She gazed up at him for several heartbeats, digesting all that. He could see she was beginning to understand his philosophy of acceptance. "You are a wise man, Sheikh Shahin Aswadi," she said at length.

"I have had a long time to ponder such things," he allowed. "And intelligent, thoughtful people to discuss them with over the years. I look forward to doing so with you."

"A *very* wise man," she continued, almost unhappily, "to tempt me with the prospect of interesting philosophical discussions, on top of your flawless body."

His smile curved. "I generally like to be on top, but in your case I could be persuaded to make an exception."

Her serious expression eased and a mutual thrum of electricity hummed through their bodies. About this, at least, they shared the same beliefs.

"You also have a very one-track mind."

He shrugged eloquently. "I am a man." But he sensed he had won her over. "Seth-Aziz awaits us, *kalila*. Will you come and meet him now?"

She swallowed. "I need to know you won't leave me."

For the first time, he didn't feel the need to hedge his answer. "I won't leave you alone. I swear."

Just as long as she didn't have betrayal on her mind. A small but necessary qualification.

"What will happen to me?" she asked, pulling him out of his sudden cascading doubts.

He refocused. "Nothing today," he assured her. "You must be taught our ways, and there are rituals to be organized. For now, your word is enough. But I must warn you, to break a promise to the demigod means death."

She drew in a calming breath and nodded. "I understand."

"Are you ready?"

"No, I'm terrified."

He took her hands in his and kissed them. "I promise, in the future you'll be glad for this day."

"I hope so," she whispered. "I truly hope so."

Chapter 15

Gemma's heart beat painfully when she found herself on her knees at the Great Western Gate for the second time that day. But this time, when Seth-Aziz bid her rise and enter the *per netjer*, she didn't bolt like a scared rabbit.

Probably a huge mistake, but there you go.

Of her own volition she was to become one of Set-Sutekh's *shemsu*. And not because she had no choice. Or because her sister had. She was unbelievably nervous and frightened over her decision. But under her very real fear, a hum of excitement stirred within her. She wanted this. She did.

She was an ethnographer, a specialist in the myth

and lore of Egypt. She'd been given an impossibly rare opportunity not only to observe a five-thousand-year-old living mythology, but also to become a part of it herself. Not to mention immortal! Although she would believe that part when she saw some hard evidence. It was difficult to accept such a thing could really be true. Then again, she had also doubted the magical spells and shape-shifting, of which she *had* seen abundant evidence.

But the real reason behind her excitement was the handsome, irresistible Sheikh Shahin. A man she felt such a deep connection with that despite his denial of returning those feelings, she was willing to give up her entire former life for the possibility of getting to know him better. And maybe change his mind.

Talk about a magic man.

She walked through the monumental gate toward him, but Seth-Aziz stepped forward to greet her instead. He was tall, taller than Shahin by a few inches, his shoulders nearly as broad. His hair was black and his eyes as well. His face was square-jawed and handsome, if a shade stern. Seth was an impressive man. Physically at least.

And powerful. Very powerful. As the vampire approached, his otherworldly power rolled over her like a heavy wave of sleepiness, a satin wind that was thick and warm, like the darkness of midnight against her skin. Oddly calm and neutral, but definitely there, ebbing and flowing like the bulge of a tide waiting for the moon to shift.

Spooky. And relaxing in an even more alarming way.

She gathered her courage as Shahin made the formal introductions.

"Welcome, Gemma," the vampire priest said, and held out his arm to her. "Let us walk."

Shahin nodded encouragingly. She made an awkward sort of bow, as she'd seen others do for him. "Yes, okay."

Hesitantly, she laid her hand over Seth-Aziz's, stifling a gasp at the wave of physical sensation that curled through her at his touch, and tried not to trip as he led her into the palace. The throng of onlookers parted, making a path for them down the wide, stone-paved corridor.

The interior of the palace was even more magnificent than its silver-gated entrance. Elegant, fire-burning torches lit their way as she and Seth-Aziz walked past soaring papyrus-shaped columns, elaborate stone-carved reliefs, gorgeous painted murals depicting scenes of the gods and secular life aboveground, luxurious tapestries hanging from the walls, and a collection of glass and precious metal objects and marble statuary that would have any museum doing cartwheels just to see, let alone own.

It was all spectacular, and gawking at everything nearly had her forgetting where she was…and that she was holding the arm of a vampire.

Shahin walked behind her, alongside the red-haired woman Gemma had noticed earlier, a priestess named Nephtys who had been introduced as Seth-Aziz's sister. She could hear her lover's steady footsteps following, reassuring her of his presence.

A few moments later they arrived at a soaringly large room flanked by more rows of glittering silver columns and headed by a raised dais where two elaborate silver thrones sat. An audience chamber, perhaps?

They went through a side door, into a more intimate room containing a scatter of tasteful furnishings and a sideboard that held plates of snacks and urns of drinks. Shahin closed the door after the four of them entered.

Seth-Aziz gestured at a cozy furniture grouping for her to sit. She waited until he took a seat on a silk-covered divan before perching on the edge of a matching chair opposite. Nephtys sat next to him.

"So, I trust by this development that you are over your misgivings about us," Seth said, his voice mild.

"Not completely," she admitted, possibly foolishly. But he didn't seem to be holding a grudge.

Thankfully, his lips twitched. "Sheikh Shahin warned us you are stubborn and skeptical."

"Family traits, I'm afraid," she said, watching as Shahin strolled to the sideboard and poured wine into four heavy silver goblets.

Seth shot her a look and the tide of energy in the room swelled noticeably. His power swirled around her, rubbing at her body like a great, invisible animal. His eyes glowed black as obsidian. "Yes, I am quite aware of that," he said, not quite as mildly.

Her sister Gillian had no doubt already tested the limits of the man's beneficence.

"Our father taught us from before we could walk to question everything in the world," Gemma explained. "He was never more pleased than when we balked at his parental orders and asked 'why' so he could lecture…er, persuade us of his reasoning, using the best Socratic method."

That seemed to smooth Seth's ruffled feathers. He smiled wryly as he accepted two goblets of wine from Shahin and passed one to Nephtys.

"How tedious for you," the priestess said, holding the goblet delicately between her fingers. "And your mother? Did she approve of such a scientific approach to child rearing?"

A prick of the old pain pierced Gemma's heart. "My mother died when I was young."

Seth took a sip of his wine, exchanged glances

with Shahin and Nephtys, who both nodded slightly, then he turned his gaze back to Gemma. She shivered, again swamped by a brush of power, and her own uncertainty.

His next words shocked her. He said, "No, I don't think she did die."

Gemma blinked. "Excuse me?"

Seth-Aziz looked directly at her and said, "The Lady Gillian found evidence in our library that your mother, Isobelle Haliday, may still be alive."

Stunned, Gemma shot to her feet. *"What?"*

Naturally she remembered Gillian's note with its similar message. The handwritten note Shahin and his ghost riders had delivered, the one that had started this whole bizarre adventure. *Incredible news—our beloved mother may still be alive. I am following every clue to find out the truth about her disappearance.* It had lived in her heart every moment since. But she never dared hoped it was really true.

"You know something about my mother?" she demanded of Seth-Aziz, forgetting momentarily with whom she was speaking.

But the demigod seemed to understand and forgive her urgency. "She was kidnapped by Haru-Re," he stated, "and taken to Petru, the *per netjer* of the Sun God, Re-Horakhti, our enemy. There is a good chance that she still lives."

Tears flooded Gemma's eyes and she made a choking sound. *Omigod!* Her mother really *could* be alive? She covered her mouth with trembling fingers, hopeless to stop the tears from trickling down her cheeks.

Two strong arms enveloped her in a warm hug. It was just what she needed. She let herself be drawn into the comfort of Shahin's embrace. "It's okay," he murmured, pulling her against his chest. "This is a good thing, yes? That she may be alive?"

Gemma gave a watery nod, burying her face in his robes. "I'm just… Oh, God, Shahin, didn't you say Khepesh is on the brink of war with Petru? My mother could be in danger! I have to get her out of there!"

"You will do nothing of the kind," Seth interjected sternly.

A thousand scattered thoughts blasted through her mind, all ending in alarm. She pulled away from Shahin and looked over at the demigod. "But I must—"

"If anyone is going to mount a rescue, it will be the captain of my guard," Seth said forcefully. "Not a woman, and certainly not a mortal. You are my subject now and you *will* obey me. Is that understood?"

She bristled and opened her mouth to object, but Shahin squeezed her shoulders, giving her an unmistakable sign to keep it shut. "Yes, I understand," she made herself say, then pressed, "But...does that mean you have plans to rescue her?"

Seth leaned back on the divan, regarding her. "That all depends on you, Miss Haliday."

Without thinking, she rushed over and flung herself down on her knees before him. "Please, Lord Seth. Tell me what I must do and I will. I'll do anything to help my mother."

"Anything?" he quietly asked.

Her heart stalled and she realized what a stupid, stupid thing that had been to say. Except...she probably *would* do anything he asked, to get her mother back safely. "Almost anything," she hedged, bowing her head respectfully.

She didn't see him smile—she was too busy studying the stone floor. But she could feel the triumph in the shift of the air in the room. A cool, tingling breeze of energy wafted over her. Shahin came to stand at her side, his hand returning to her shoulder.

"You know what I want, Gemma," Seth said.

"No, I don't," she insisted.

But her sinking heart told her she did. There was only one possibility.

"Your sister," he said softly. "I want Josslyn."

Her heart squeezed in torment.

"Will you tell us where she is?" he asked.

She swallowed heavily. *Her mother or her sister.* An impossible choice!

Oh, God, what should she do?

Seth might be an all-powerful demigod, but he didn't know Gemma, thought Shahin. Seth believed he could intimidate her, but Shahin knew better.

He was very afraid she would do something very foolish in response to the high priest's not-so-subtle ploy. He held his breath as she rose to her feet with as much dignity as any mortal could muster.

"Blackmail is unworthy of you and your god," she announced to Seth unflinchingly. "As is forcing a cruel choice like that."

Ouch.

But well played. Shahin had to stop himself from smiling.

Nephtys did it for him. "I agree," the priestess said approvingly, with a look of reprove for her brother. "You know very well you have every intention of rescuing Isobelle Haliday when we invade Petru. Why not simply tell the girl and win her over? She is much more likely to give you the information you seek if she trusts you."

Seth scowled, while Gemma looked nonplussed.

"Is it true?" she asked. "You already have plans to rescue my mother?"

"Yes," Seth admitted grudgingly. "Along with all of Ray's other captives. But it's far from certain we'll win this war or even invade Petru at all. In fact, it's more likely we won't. You shouldn't get your hopes up."

Gemma blinked, apparently surprised speechless.

Shahin said, "We will naturally do what we can to right the recent wrongs at Petru. As I said, here at Khepesh we have long abandoned the practice of taking mortals against their will."

"And yet you plan to do exactly that with my sister," she pointed out.

"We planned *your* capture as well, Gemma," Shahin reminded her. "And yet here you are, by your own choice. Why do you think your sister will react any differently to us than you did? Or to the man who has chosen her for himself, as I did you?"

She blinked again and a flush of pink stained her cheeks. Then her gaze darted to Seth and back again.

"Because he is a vampire?" Shahin asked, reading her thoughts. It wasn't difficult.

She bit her lip, but before she could answer, Nephtys said, "I think, dear brother, you should give Miss Haliday a taste of what it's like to be with a vampire. Then maybe she'll understand that a small blood sacrifice is a small price to pay for the pleasures her sister will enjoy every night."

Shahin straightened like a shot. "My lord, I—"

But Seth waved him off as he rose lithely from the divan and approached Gemma. "Would you like that?" he asked.

"No!" she squeaked and slid behind Shahin's back for protection, clinging to his arm. "Thank you," she added belatedly. As if that was going to help.

Shahin narrowed his eyes at Seth-Aziz. The beginnings of a temblor rumbled the floor under his feet. "She is mine. You gifted her to me."

"I have no intention of taking your woman," Seth assured him. "But by keeping me from her sister she has delayed my feeding. I only seek remedy." His face took on a look of calculation. "We could share magic. That way all three of us would see a benefit."

Shahin's jaw dropped in stunned surprise. He met Nephtys's rounded eyes and they exchanged a look of silent astonishment.

This was an unheard of privilege.

In Shahin's lifetime, Seth had not shared magic with any man. There had been only two vampires left in existence by the time Shahin became an immortal, and neither one enjoyed bedplay with other men. Of course, Shahin didn't either. Seth also tended to stick to one bed partner at a time. As did Shahin. To be honest, he wasn't sure how he felt about sharing his woman, even with his lord and leader. No, he did. He would not countenance it.

But sharing magic was different. Shahin would be making love with Gemma as Seth fed on her. In ancient times, it was a way for the demigod to bestow special favor upon a male subject. A man would be a fool to turn down such an honor and its attendant breath-stealing pleasures.

Finally, Nephtys broke through her astonishment, smiled and said into the taut silence, "Sharing magic. Oh, what a lovely idea!"

Gemma sidled out from behind Shahin's back. "What is that?" she asked warily.

All eyes turned to her. Shahin could feel the dark roil of erotic male power purl through the room as he and Seth contemplated the intriguing possibilities.

He could also feel Gemma's growing trepidation.

Step by careful step, she started backing away from them, like a lamb from a trio of hungry wolves. She sought out each of their gazes, one by one. And finally whispered, "What the hell are you talking about?"

Chapter 16

"No." Gemma shook her head vehemently after Shahin's explanation of what it meant to share magic.

Nephtys wondered what planet the men were living on to think Gemma would ever go along with this idea.

"*I'll* be the one making love with you," Shahin said. "You'll barely notice he's there."

Nephtys watched Gemma's expression run the gamut from incredulous to petrified and back again. The poor girl had no clue what would really happen. Or if she did, the idea scared her witless. Nephtys couldn't really blame her. Gemma had only just learned of the existence of vampires. The idea took some getting used to. Let alone this.

It was a long time ago, but Nephtys could still remember in vivid detail the full-body shock when she'd found out about vampires…and not in a theoretical way either, but as Haru-Re's fangs descended and sank into her as he took her virginity. It had been equal parts thrilling and terrifying. Okay, a lot more terrifying. And not a first time a woman was ever likely to forget.

The kind of introduction to a vampire's kiss that the men were contemplating would be nearly as shocking and intimate as her own had been.

"It wouldn't be a full feeding," Seth assured Gemma. He lifted a hand, beckoning her to take it. "Just a taste. So you can see what it's like. For your sister."

"No!" She snatched both her hands behind her back.

Nephtys spoke up. "The kiss of a vampire is something many women would pay much to experience," she told her. "Immortals are used to the enhanced pleasures that love spells bring to physical encounters, but even immortals vie for the chance to be chosen as my brother's sacrifice."

"Sacrifice?" Gemma squeaked, though Nephtys could tell that a small, unwilling part of her was beginning to become intrigued. But not enough to

let herself be bitten. And she didn't know the half of it.

"Do you know what it's like?" Nephtys ventured. It would be impossible for an ethnographer such as Gemma not to have heard the myriad stories and legends told by the local villagers.

Gemma's cheeks flooded with color. So she had.

Nephtys hid a smile. It was sweet how she kept blushing, especially when Shahin looked at her in a certain way. As he was doing now. A look filled with heat and stark want.

"I understand it's...pleasurable," Gemma answered.

Pleasurable was, indeed, the understatement of the century. Eating ice cream was pleasurable. Being bitten by a vampire was like being engulfed by a tsunami of sexual excitement, pleasure and satisfaction.

Shahin was looking anticipatory—if a bit shaken—at the suggestion Seth had made to share magic with him. She assumed the latter was because of the intimacy of the act with another man.

But Shahin didn't actually have to touch Seth if he didn't want to. Nor did Gemma, really, other than to let the vampire sink his fangs into some body part not in use by Shahin as they made love. The magic of doing the two simultaneously was that

Seth would feel what Shahin's body was feeling, and add his vampiric sexual powers to the mix, thereby amplifying everyone's pleasure a hundredfold. For a straight man, it was the only way to experience the explosive sexuality of being a vampire, or being with a vampire.

The powerful magic could also potentially bind a woman's affections. Whether it was Seth or another, she could be bound to the man making love to her during the vampire's bite. If Gemma released her will and succumbed to the magic, as many women did in the heat of the moment, she would never want any other man than Shahin. She would be loyal and true to him alone, and he would never have to worry about her betraying him. He was surely thinking about that part, too.

However, it was all academic. If Nephtys was reading Gemma correctly, sensual tsunami or no, she would not go for it.

Seth stepped closer to her and she took a step backward. Shahin blocked her retreat. Her back collided with his chest and he stood his ground, slipping his arms around her waist from behind, holding her loosely in place.

Seth smiled at her. "Don't be afraid, my pet. Nothing will happen if you don't want it to. You must give your permission for a blood sacrifice."

"I won't," Gemma said. But her voice was soft

and breathy and no longer quite so adamant. Fine trembles sifted visibly through her body.

Nephtys was sure she was still too frightened to consent. It didn't help that the men were acting like Apis bulls, when the situation called for the delicate feline touch of Bastet.

"Never mind," Nephtys interjected briskly, salvaging the situation from potential disaster. She rose from the divan, grasped Gemma's hands and pulled her away from the men. "You can all discuss this later. It's time we ladies got ready for the banquet."

The two men frowned at her, annoyed that their attempt at seduction was interrupted before it could even get off the ground.

Gemma looked taken aback. "Banquet?"

"In your honor," Shahin said, recovering first. He picked up his wine goblet and lifted it in a toast. "The immortals want to welcome Khepesh's newest initiate into the *per netjer*."

Gemma's lips parted. "But how did they know? I agreed to enter the palace less than an hour ago."

"There were quite a few witnesses." He shrugged boyishly. "Any excuse for a party, which can be organized in mere minutes when called for. A new follower is the best reason of all to celebrate."

"Oh, that's…um, very nice." But she still looked unsure.

"Let's see…" Nephtys made a whirling motion with her finger for Gemma to twirl around, and surveyed her critically. The emerald dress she had on was beautiful but not nearly formal enough for her official welcome. "Come with me. We'll go to the temple and find something more suitable for you to wear."

Gemma shot a worried glance at Shahin. "Oh, but—"

"Go," he urged. "Nephtys will take good care of you. I'll see you in a little while at the feast. I promise."

The young woman's face paled a bit, but after a short hesitation, she let Nephtys lead her to the door. There, Nephtys paused and glanced back at the men. What she saw made her smile. The look on Shahin's face as he watched Gemma leave the room said everything she wanted to know.

Thank Isis. At long last, the man was clearly in love.

"She's pretty," Seth said as the door closed behind the two women. "And spirited. I like her."

A spike of jealousy shot through Shahin. He'd seen Gemma weakening as Seth had poured on the charm. Was it honest, or had the vampire used glamour to try and influence her decision?

No, his friend wouldn't do that. Seth was not

interested in Gemma. He was only using this as a way to get to Josslyn, his true desire.

"Yes, she is," Shahin agreed politely. "Almost as pretty as Nephtys."

Seth smiled. "They do make quite the striking pair of bookends with all that wild red hair. They could be sisters."

Shahin grunted. "Which is one reason I want to keep her as far away from Haru-Re as possible."

"Yes, it *would* get awkward if he took a fancy to her." Seth strolled over to the sideboard and topped up his wine. "But you're okay sharing her with me, yes?" He raised an enquiring brow.

"Her blood, you mean?" Shahin inclined his head in a nod. "With her consent. Just as long as it goes no further." But he was torn and his voice must have betrayed him.

Seth's lip curled. "Afraid she'll be vamp-struck?"

Hell, as long as it was out there on the table… "Most women are, after being with you," Shahin pointed out. "But be warned, I have no intention of giving her up."

"Nor I of taking her," Seth assured him. "I know enough of my destiny that she isn't an intimate part of it. My sole interest at this point is Josslyn. Nephtys thinks her vision was probably of her and not Gillian."

Shahin nodded. "Which would make sense, all things considered."

"I just wish we could convince Gemma I mean her sister no harm. It would be a great relief to have my future consort here in my care and not somewhere out there hiding from things she doesn't understand."

"Hopefully tonight will do it."

Seth made a noise of agreement, then regarded him thoughtfully. "What does it feel like?"

Shahin shot him a puzzled look. "What?"

"Being in love."

His mouth dropped open in surprise. "I couldn't possibly say."

"Indeed?"

Just then, there was a knock at the door and a messenger appeared. "My lord, the Lord High Council requests a quick word before the festivities."

"Tell him I'll be there in a moment." The messenger disappeared, and Seth turned back to Shahin. "In any case, we're agreed on our course of action tonight?"

Shahin met the high priest's eyes in an exchange of perfect understanding. They would work their magic on Gemma together, and each would gain what he wanted.

"Yes," Shahin said. "In complete agreement."

* * *

Shahin left the audience chamber still startled by Seth's question. Why in Hades would he ask *him* about being in love?

Surely, he didn't think Shahin was in *love* with Gemma?

In love? *Him?*

The idea was completely absurd.

Dismissing the thought, he strode to his apartments in the residential wing that was reserved for Khepesh's leaders. He was a man of simple needs and his rooms weren't as lavish as many others, but they were a good deal more luxurious than his Bedouin tent at the oasis.

His furnishings were simple but elegant, the decor understated, the magic powerful. The apartment consisted of a generous living room and dining room, a minimalist kitchen and a large bedroom with a walk-in closet and an opulent en suite bath. The focal point of the bedroom was a tall, massive bed—the place he did most of his entertaining.

Tonight would be no exception.

But for the first time, there would be three people in the bed. If Gemma consented. At the thought of her, his heart quickened. A feeling of elation flooded through him.

He wanted this. Not just for the immense pleasure, or for the honor it bestowed upon him, or even to convince Gemma to help Seth find Josslyn. But because of the possibility that Gemma could be bound to him forever through the act. The idea filled him with an acute possessiveness. He wanted to own her affections with an unbreakable certainty. To know without question she would be loyal to him alone and would never betray him.

Only then would he feel safe enough to allow himself to fall in love. That was *his* fantasy.

He went to his closet and chose his favorite robes, those in deep scarlet and black, the colors favored by Set-Sutekh. Normally on festive occasions, the men of Khepesh wore colorful breeches, boots and tunics fashioned in the style of the desert nomad, along with a floor-length, flowing *bisht* of the finest silk. This evening, Shahin decided to dispense with the tunic. His bare chest would be prominently displayed under the open cloak, a statement to all that he was out to impress his chosen lady. The immortals of Khepesh were a randy lot and would appreciate such a blatantly erotic gesture. Their speculation would raise the level of sensual energy flowing through the room, which would already be high in celebration. It couldn't help but have a seductive effect on Gemma.

He wanted her in his bed tonight. And not alone.

He wondered what she would wear to the feast.

Nephtys had heard their plans for tonight and given her blessing to the sharing of magic. She would no doubt dress Gemma in something provocative. With any luck, she would also cast a spell of physical awareness over the garment. All to enhance the mood and their chances of success.

After making sure the bedroom was well prepared for his guests, Shahin bathed and dressed and headed for the grand hall.

As always, the pure darkness of the midnight-black banquet hall was pierced by the sparkle of ten thousand tiny candles placed on the long tables, and reflected by the million glittering diamonds that spangled the void of the ceiling above in a pattern of the stars of the Milky Way. Set-Sutekh was the Lord of the Night Sky, Guardian of the Dark Universe, and this room did him true homage.

Unencumbered by the dimness of the room, Shahin worked his way through the crowd of *shemsu* that had gathered in haste to celebrate the *per netjer*'s newest initiate. He greeted his many friends and received congratulations and hearty backslapping for his role in her acquisition. He felt proud of her and was eager to show her off to them.

And that she belonged to him.

"What's this?" one of his spies said, indicating his bare chest with a grin. "The woman has you shedding your clothes already? I can't wait to see this beauty. Maybe I'll steal her from you!"

"You can try," Shahin returned with an answering grin that in no way masked the note of cold warning in his tone. He felt the aura of power around his body increase, attracting even more interest. Something was up and they all knew it. An atmosphere of heightened sensuality started to brew and grow, making the air in the hall heavy and fragrant with the expectation of sex. The room sizzled with anticipation.

"You've already claimed her, I hear," one of his old lovers said with a moue. She and her pretty companions pressed in around him, touching his arms and his naked chest with questing hands. The scent of passion swirled temptingly about them. "Does this mean the legendary Sheikh Shahin no longer accepts visitors to his tent?"

He gave them a broad smile and let them touch. He enjoyed female attention as much as the next man. "That depends on how much she amuses me," he answered with a wink.

"I'm not too worried," another said with a coy slant of her eyes. "No woman has ever held your attention for more than a precious few nights."

"It's true," he admitted, though not for the reasons she believed. He leaned in and murmured to her in a stage whisper, "It is difficult to find a woman who can match my appetites."

Although last night came damn close. Tonight should prove even better.

"Perhaps you need more than one woman at a time," a third suggested saucily, putting her arms around the first two and posturing. A wave of unconcealed female invitation washed over him, brimming with promise.

He laughed. "An intriguing thought," he allowed. *If only they knew.* But he wasn't interested in these women. There was only one woman he wanted in his bed tonight or for the foreseeable future, despite his warning to her of boredom. He was already aroused thinking of what would transpire after the feast.

He kept walking, slowly making his way to his accustomed place on the dais at the front of the room. He had just taken his seat when Seth-Aziz entered the room and ascended the elaborate silver throne in its place of honor at the high table. Tonight, Nephtys occupied the other, smaller throne.

The crowd rose and paid their respects to the demigod, chanting a song of greeting to their revered high priest. The melody was beautiful and dissonant at the same time, and the words carried an undertone of excitement and pleasure. Seth was a firm and commanding leader, but he was respected and well loved by his people. He beamed back at them and accepted their greeting, making a short speech conveying his happiness over Gemma becoming one of the *shemsu*, and urging them to make her welcome. His rare smile was genuine, but Shahin couldn't help notice how very tired Seth's eyes looked. He really needed to feed on mortal blood soon. It was a good thing they were sharing magic tonight. Until Josslyn was fetched to Khepesh, Gemma was the only one within reach who could give him the boost he needed.

Shahin had a brief stab of worry. Would the vampire be able to stop once he'd tasted Gemma's blood? Or would the hunger take over…? If so, what would happen? How much blood could he take before she—

No.

Shahin shook off the disturbing thought and refocused on the ceremony at hand.

The sweet chords of a lyre and the rattle of a drum sounded from the other side of the room, and a luminescent moon welled up above the entry portal and shone a beam down on the center aisle. The two temple *shemats* stepped side-by-side into the beam of light and began a stately procession toward the dais.

They were followed by Gemma.

Shahin's woman.

His breath caught. Clad in a shimmering, body-hugging ancient-style gown of diaphanous silver and violet, she looked utterly gorgeous.

And more than a little overwhelmed. Her wide eyes lifted, skittering about the hall. He willed her to pick him out of the crowd. She did. Their gazes caught and held for several long, breathless heartbeats.

His chest squeezed.

And that was the moment he knew.

It didn't matter that he didn't trust her completely.

It didn't matter how much the idea of giving his heart to her terrified him.

And it didn't matter if the magic tonight did not bind her to him as he hoped.

He suddenly knew with every fiber of his being that she was the one he wanted by his side.

For all time.

She was *his*.

And he would never let her go.

Never.

Chapter 17

Gemma walked toward the front of the banquet hall, transfixed by her lover's gaze. In a matter of seconds, she saw his expression go from lazy arrogance to proud admiration to primitive possessiveness.

He wanted her. It was written in his posture, in the set of his mouth, in the way he gripped his goblet. His desire was nothing new. But she sensed something different now, a kind of prowling masculine energy emanating from every inch of him that went deeper, beyond lust. The look in his black eyes was harder, the tight line of his sculpted lips far more determined than she'd ever seen before.

His laser-like regard was like a bird of prey focusing in on the unfortunate animal he was planning to devour. Or on the fortunate female he had decided to take as his mate.

Did hawks mate for life?

A shivering thrill danced down Gemma's body. Heavens, she hoped so!

Which was when a blinding insight hit her head-on, like a freight train from hell.

Omigod.

She *was* in love with him!

The notorious Sheikh Shahin, captain of the death warriors.

Immortal shape-shifter.

She loved him. And there was nothing she wanted more than to spend an eternity with him.

Once again, she felt her whole world turn upside down. Fantasizing about the man was one thing, even emotional connection and lust for him. But *love?*

Her knees turned to noodles and she started to stumble. Invisible hands grasped her and she knew instinctively that Shahin had reached out with his magic to catch her when she would have fallen. Would he catch her heart as willingly?

A chaos of thoughts and feelings rushed through her as she continued the endless walk down the center aisle to the raised platform where he awaited her.

The man she loved.

Lord! How had this *happened?*

He was still watching her intently. He didn't smile. In fact, he looked like a thundercloud about to burst. Obviously, he wasn't pleased. But why? Because the love in her eyes had betrayed her true feelings for him? Or because he'd seen her shock and dismay over the terrifying truth she'd finally admitted to herself?

No doubt the former. Shahin had told her in no uncertain terms he didn't need or want a woman in his life other than a temporary bed partner. That her very presence here at Khepesh—and in his bed— was just a by-product of Seth's quest for Josslyn.

That hurt more than was rational. After all, what did it matter that the *per netjer* hadn't sought her out for her own sake, not as an extension of their desire for her sister? Gemma knew they'd eventually come to like and respect her on her own merit. People always did. *Eventually.* Nevertheless, it stung. A lot.

Story of her life.

She took a deep breath and shook off Shahin's invisible grip. She could do this on her own. She *would* do this on her own. She'd chosen this path and she would make the best of it. Alone, if she had to—regardless of her feelings for him. And regardless of how he felt about her—or didn't.

She lifted her chin and halted at the foot of the low stairs ascending the dais, avoiding Shahin's steely looks.

Seth-Aziz gazed beneficently down at her as Nephtys made a formal, ritualistic introduction. Seth then greeted her warmly and bid her ascend the stairs. When she reached the top he kissed her cheeks and smiled.

"Turn, Gemma," he said, gesturing to the gathering of immortals below them, "and be welcomed by your new brethren."

As she turned, a haunting chant began, sung in a strange, hypnotic harmony by the swaying crowd. A delicate swirl of positive energy wrapped around her, enveloping her in a gossamer quilt of goodwill and pleasurable physical sensation. As they sang, she could feel their curiosity…and their anticipation. A thrum of excitement began within their bodies, blossoming and spreading from person to person, erotic, contagious.

It was an incredible feeling. Surreal. Magical. Unbelievably arousing.

Nephtys had told her celebrations at Khepesh were filled with sensual indulgences of all kinds. Food, drink. Sex. It was expected that she would choose one of the *shemsu* to spend the night with.

Naturally, everyone presumed it would be Shahin. But it was her choice.

She looked out over the sea of handsome men before her, and felt the physical caress of sexual suggestion, as if each one of them was reaching out to entice her, tempting her to pick him as her lover for the night. She wished to hell that any of them attracted her even half as much as Shahin. Life would be so much easier.

"Gemma." She heard the rumble of her lover's deep voice in her ear, as though he stood right next to her. "You are mine, *kalila*. Come to me."

She glanced back at him. Saw the command written in the stark shadows of his face and the tautness of his muscles. Her body gave an involuntary shiver. There was no denying he was a powerful man. Very powerful. It was nearly impossible to refuse him anything he asked of her.

This time she didn't even try.

She followed her heart. And went to the man she loved.

The celebration lasted for hours. There were speeches and formal toasts of greeting by dozens of the *shemsu*, women as well as men. After the first few, Gemma was glowing with happiness, imbued with an overwhelming feeling of welcome and acceptance.

Perhaps they really *did* want her here.

But did Shahin?

When she'd come to him, his expression had been impossible to decipher, but then he'd wrapped his hand behind her neck and kissed her long and hard. Thoroughly enough that the crowd below had started to stir. She'd felt a thick wave of sultry energy purl through the room as he kissed her, making her flesh heat and her skin tingle with arousal. It was the kind of kiss that could conquer a woman's will to be cautious. A claiming kiss.

But was it a claim just for tonight…or for always? He gave her no clue as he handed her into her seat at the high table.

As the feast was brought in on huge platters, ethereal music began to play in the background, soft and evocative. Shahin sat next to her, Seth on his throne on her other side, Nephtys next to Seth on the smaller throne. The food and the wine were sublime, each dish more delicious than the last. Throughout the long meal, the four of them shared the bounty with each other, passing their most succulent bits for the others to taste. They laughed and chatted, and Gemma found she genuinely liked the high priest and his beautiful sister. Shahin was quieter, always watching her like a hawk, but even he managed to smile and have a good time.

Even without all the wine, Gemma was dizzy enough from the flow of sensual energy that swirled and eddied through the grand hall that she tried not to drink too much. But with each new vintage that arrived at the table, the men offered her sips from their goblets, and soon she was feeling warm and alive, and buzzing with a kind of whole-body pleasure.

It was the weirdest thing, but a real sense of homecoming settled about her like an old, favorite quilt. Like this was exactly where she belonged. In this place. With these people. And especially this man.

Now if she could just convince *him* of that.

After everyone had finished eating, the tables below magically disappeared and there was dancing. It was a kind of partner dancing she'd never seen before. Sensual and beautiful, the bodies of the immortals blended and swayed to the music, forming the most extraordinary patterns, like a living kaleidoscope, and making soft brushing sounds with their feet on the floor. They touched and kissed as part of the dances, and clothes were shed as the hours grew later and later. It was the sexiest celebration she'd ever witnessed.

Shahin asked her more than once if she'd like to join in the dancing, but she demurred. "I'll wait until I can learn the steps," she told him, nevertheless wishing she already did. She would love to be floating in his bare arms, part of the sensual flow of bodies.

"I'll teach you," he said with a languorous smile, and leaned over to give her a soft kiss.

"I'd like that," she said, her body giving a shiver of pleasure at the taste of him on her tongue. Perhaps later they would indulge in a different kind of dance all on their own.

Sensing her pleasure, he deepened the kiss. She opened to him and desire swept through her in a warm flood. She loved it when he kissed her. Loved when he touched her. She yearned for him to sweep her against his hard body and make love to her all night long.

Reading her mind, he lifted his mouth from hers and murmured, "I want you under me. Let's go to my rooms."

At his bold declaration, her nipples pebbled and a surge of stark want raced through her. She nodded and they rose to leave.

He took her hand and guided her down the steps of the dais and through the crowded room. The dancing people smiled and twirled about them as they walked, blowing kisses and making her blush with their sultry, knowing looks. Erotic energy spilled from them like heat from an oven, filling her body with an overwhelming need for Shahin's intimate touch.

She had no memory of how they reached his rooms, but suddenly they were inside an elegant apartment, standing in his salon, still kissing.

"You are so incredibly beautiful tonight," he murmured, running his hand over the silken fabric of her form-fitting gown. "This is the perfect color for you."

She flushed with pleasure at his compliment and smiled up at him. "You're not so bad yourself. I love the no-shirt look." She brushed her fingers over the smooth skin of his chest, feeling the hard discs of his male nipples.

He gave a low, half-lidded hum and let his robe slide off his shoulders. He tossed it aside in a move that should have looked feminine but just made him even more commanding.

He touched a strap of her gown with a curve of his lips. "Now you."

"Hardly fair," she said, fingering the waistband of his pants. "I've got nothing on under mine."

The curve broadened. "So much the better."

"You first."

"You know it's not real, yes?"

She blinked. "What isn't?"

"Your dress. It's just an illusion conjured by Nephtys for the occasion. A real gown of such exquisite fabric would have been too troublesome to come up with on this short notice."

She looked down at her dress, which seemed completely solid and genuine to her. "Really?"

"I could simply make it disappear." He grinned.

She pretended to be aghast. But before she could form a proper comeback, a masculine voice behind her said, "What a delightful prospect."

She whirled to see Seth standing between her and the closed entry door. His power rolled over her like a cool, spicy fragrance. "Seth-Aziz! How did you get in here?"

He gave her an indulgent smile. "I am a demigod, my dear. Doors and walls are no obstacle for me." He shrugged eloquently. "Besides, I was invited."

She turned back to Shahin uncertainly. "What's going on, Shahin? Why is he here?" But she had a nervous feeling she knew exactly why. Nervous and…just a little aroused. Seth-Aziz was a very attractive man and had been utterly charming and charismatic at the banquet.

Shahin took her hands. "We talked about this, *kalila*. Seth has come to share magic with us."

She licked her lips, her heartbeat kicking up, remembering Shahin's explanation of what that entailed. "I'm pretty sure I said no."

"We thought you might reconsider," Seth said, suddenly standing right behind her. She could feel the intensity of his power rub against the bare skin of her back like a big, sleek cat. A quiver shimmered up her spine. And her denial froze in her throat.

What they were suggesting was outrageous. Two men in bed with her, one making love with her, the other drinking her blood! Earlier, the prospect had scared her witless. After getting to know him better, she had to admit she was no longer terrified of the vampire. But could she really do it?

"We felt your sense of happiness and acceptance during the feast," Shahin said, putting his arms around her waist.

Seth touched her shoulders lightly from behind. "We felt your desire to become one of us."

"One *with* us," Shahin murmured low in her ear, pulling her closer.

"We want you to tell Josslyn what it's like to be here in Khepesh. What it's like to be with me," Seth said.

She was tempted. *Lord,* was she tempted! The stories she'd heard of a vampire's kiss were enough to spark any woman's longing to sample such incredible pleasures. But... She swallowed and turned back to face Seth. "If my sister truly is meant to become your consort, how can you ask me to do this? Touching you would be—" several words came to mind, but she settled on "—disloyal."

He smiled. "And I would never betray Shahin by allowing his woman to do so. Not in the way you mean. The pleasure you feel will be all about the man you are making love with—Shahin, not me. Despite the nearness of our bodies, I will simply be taking blood. Nothing sexual—other than the magic."

The overwhelming male power that saturated the room intensified, feeling like flames of passion licking at her most intimate places. Her willpower wavered precariously.

Shahin turned her in his arms and tightened his hold on her. "I'm glad you don't want him that way, Gemma," he murmured, and lowered his lips to hers. "It pleases me."

She didn't have the strength to resist his kiss. Or the rest of it either. The temptation of the pleasures being offered was too great. After a heartbeat's hesitation, she opened for him and leaned into his body. She could feel Seth hovering at her back, barely touching, but enough to feel the arousing caress of his otherworldly energy.

The force of Shahin's kiss conveyed the elation he felt at her surrender. When he lifted his lips, she was breathless, boneless in his arms. A palpable wave of intense desire spilled from his body into hers. She shivered, softly moaning his name. "Are you bespelling me?" she asked.

"No. It's the magic you're feeling."

With a smile, he lifted her fingers to his mouth

and slowly kissed the tips of them one by one by one. Then he drew her hand over her shoulder and pressed it into Seth's waiting grasp.

She inhaled sharply. "Shahin, what—"

"Shh, *kalila*. Just enjoy what you're feeling."

The vampire brushed his lips over her knuckles as Shahin leaned down to kiss her again. They both took their time, Shahin kissing her mouth deeply, exploring it with wet, languid strokes that she could feel intensely between her legs. Seth gathered her fingers in his and flicked his tongue over the soft pad of the first one, then enveloped it with his mouth and gently sucked, tonguing the tip. At the same time, both men stroked her body with their magical power until she was again breathless and boneless, trembling with a need for something she didn't quite understand.

That was when she felt the subtle scrape of fangs against her finger.

She gasped as an involuntary convulsion of pleasure seized her body. The hard points of her nipples dragged against Shahin's chest as she squirmed.

Unable to stop herself, she half turned in his arms and watched with terrified fascination as Seth's fangs descended, long and lethally sharp. She felt the liquid pull of the vampire's sexual power sweep through her, making her blood slow and grow, oh, so heavy in her veins. She was drowning in pleasure. Her body was shaking so badly she could barely stand.

Because it was obvious what would come next.

God help her. She should stop him! But she couldn't make herself do it.

She wanted to know what it was like.

Shahin wound his fist in her hair and forced her around to face him, commanding her attention back to him. He angled his tall frame over her and covered her mouth with his.

Suddenly a sharp prick pierced her finger. She jumped and shivered deeply as a hot, sexual pull shot through her whole body.

Shahin groaned into her mouth, his fingers digging into her flesh as he must have felt it, too.

A low rumble came from Seth's throat. "Gemma, look at me."

She glanced back. He was holding her finger up. A tiny, perfect bead of blood was forming on the very tip. The vampire watched hungrily as it bloomed and swelled, then tore his eyes back to her, pinioning her with his obsidian gaze.

"Do I have your permission?" he asked, his voice like the rough tear of velvet in the stillness of the room. "May I take your sacrifice?"

Chapter 18

Shahin's insides were on fire with a ravening hunger. *The vampire's thirst for blood.* Shahin needed Gemma to say yes.

Even more, Seth needed her to say yes.

As Shahin held her tight, her body undulated in his arms, as if seeking relief from her own deep, deep need. He could sense the battle between her intense physical craving and the emotional reluctance that still lingered within her.

"One drop," Shahin coaxed. He had to have this; to experience the explosive sex he could feel prowling in the magic that roiled around the three of them. "Let him have his taste, *kalila*. What could it hurt?"

She still hesitated, but her breath shuddered. She wanted to say yes, but was afraid.

Shahin ran his hand up her body to her breast and rubbed his thumb over the stiff nipple, at the same time sending a magical pulse of desire hurtling through her. She gasped and bowed in his arms, feeling the impact of his spell. He turned her head to kiss her hard.

He had never felt anything as intensely as he was now feeling everything around him. Every sensual movement of Gemma's lush body against him, every agonizing pang of this new, voracious hunger. Every rapacious carnal need of his own flesh; every wrenching pain of Seth's violent need for blood.

Seth pressed in close to her and asked again, his voice a tightly controlled whisper, "May I, Gemma?"

His fangs flashed white against his dusky lips, eerily reflecting the flickering light of the torch sconces on the walls.

Shahin could feel the out-of-control pounding of her heart, her quickened breath, the quiver of unfulfilled need between her legs. Last night, he had learned the responses of her body to his lovemaking. She was close to coming now, her flesh finally succumbing to the erotic powers of the vampire and the spell of desire he himself had cast upon her.

She tore her mouth from his and looked back at Seth in desperation. Shahin could feel her trepidation over what was about to happen, but even more, he could feel her body's aching desire for it.

"Yes," she relented on a soft moan. She squeezed her eyes shut. "Yes! Take the drop."

Seth's power swelled like a storm cloud, filling the room. But it did not let loose in a torrent, as Shahin expected. Slowly, with tightly leashed control, Seth extended his tongue and barely touched the pad of her finger, rolling the bead of blood expertly onto the tip. As he brought the scarlet drop into his mouth, he smiled in blissful relief.

Instantly, Gemma's body convulsed. She cried out, gasping hard as she shattered in Shahin's arms. He held her as her knees gave out and she dissolved in a deluge of pleasure, her head thrown back against his shoulder.

His own desire flared to a desperate crescendo, egged on by the vampire's enjoyment of his coppery morsel, but he did not let himself release. Nor did Seth. This wasn't about them seeking satisfaction.

Not yet.

Shahin turned Gemma and held her until she came back from that place of unconscious ecstasy.

"My God," she whispered hoarsely when she finally opened her eyes. "My *God*."

"Good?" he asked with a smile.

Seth moved away from them, going to the bar to pour himself a drink. Shahin didn't know if the distance was to remove the temptation of taking more blood, or if he really did have such command over his darker instincts that he could be unaffected by taking just one drop. His need for more had certainly felt immense to Shahin.

Gemma glanced over at Seth, looking, if possible, even more frightened than she had before. "That was...truly amazing," she said, her eyes troubled with a muddle of disbelief and...was it *craving* Shahin saw?

"That was just a tiny taste," Shahin said. More and better lay ahead for all of them. *He hoped.* He dropped his hold on her and started backing slowly toward the bedroom. He held out his hand to her, beckoning. "Just the beginning, *kalila*. Come. I want your body under mine."

She didn't move but stole a glance at Seth, who was now propped against the bar, drink in hand.

"Forget Seth," Shahin ordered her. "*I'm* the one who'll be inside you, not him."

She gave a little shiver. "Other than his fangs," she reminded him.

Seth smiled behind his glass. "Was it so bad?" he asked her.

She closed her eyes and again that warring mixture of need and caution cut across her face. "I've heard…the bite can be addictive."

"Not to every woman," Seth returned. "And in this case, because of the shared magic, if you do become addicted, it will be to the touch of your lover, not me."

Shahin thought he detected a slight quail in her stance at that. He himself was shocked by the revelation. "Is that true?"

Seth nodded. "But Gemma strikes me as a strong woman with no propensity for total dependence on a man. I would be very surprised if she falls victim to such a weakness."

She opened her eyes. "This is not a good idea," she said hoarsely, and glanced at Shahin uncomfortably.

Under his feet an earth tremor began to rumble. The thought of her needing him like that filled him with an overwhelming and primitive need for her unconditional surrender.

Now.

"On the contrary," he refuted, "it's a very good idea."

It wasn't fair to bespell her, but fuck fair. He wanted her. He wanted her addicted to his presence, to his touch, helpless against the longing to be with him. So he could trust she would never betray him.

He drilled his gaze into hers, whispered a spell and compelled her to come to him. The shaking of the room increased.

Her body obeyed but she knew exactly what he was doing. "You're a bastard," she whispered as he pulled her into his grasp.

"But not a vampire," he returned. "Addiction can work both ways, *kalila*. Perhaps it is *I* who shall fall prey."

He had no idea if that was true or not, but it suddenly struck him as a real possibility. He glanced over her head at Seth, but *that* bastard just smiled and poured himself another drink.

So it was a risk.

Shahin didn't care.

He swept Gemma up into his arms and stalked into the bedroom, each footstep causing the floor to jolt. He deposited her in the middle of the bed and with a *crack* snapped his fingers over her. Her gown dissolved in a shimmering flash and disappeared.

She was indeed naked under it.

She sucked in a breath and jerked her gaze up to watch him walk to the foot of the bed. Her eyes were turbulent with emotion. Anger?

It didn't matter. She was *his*.

He'd compelled her into the bedroom, but he would not make her stay. He released his spell. Would she run?

A steady rumble churned through the air, giving voice to the tension between them.

She didn't flee. Instead, she leaned back on his pillows and regarded him with lashes lowered to a slant. His answering smile felt as edgy as the blade of his scimitar. He stripped off the rest of his clothes and stood for a brief, pregnant moment, letting her take in the fury of his arousal. He was thick and long as a granite column.

She had climaxed. *He had not.*

Nor had Seth. The door opened, then clicked closed. The power of Seth's presence rolled over them, restrained, simmering, infinitely patient in its voracious hunger.

Her breasts rose and fell, her chest flushed with vivid color. She licked her lips, hesitated, then with a slow, deliberate movement, she parted her thighs for Shahin.

His cock was so ready.

In a single fluid motion he was on the bed and on top of her. He gripped her under her knees and spread her wide for his entry. He captured her eyes.

"Do it," she answered his unspoken question. Her pulse was pounding so fast and hard he could see it beating in her throat like the wings of a bird. "Do all of it," she cried.

And he plunged into her.

Shahin filled Gemma and kept filling her. She was sure she would come apart from the sheer pleasure of feeling him swell inside her. She forgot all about Seth.

Shahin hilted, withdrew and scythed into her again. Hard. She cried out again and again as he thrust into her over and over. Last night, he'd been a thoughtful and inventive lover, but this time there was no finesse, no pretense, no holding back…and no chance for regrets over what she was doing. Just good, hard, bone-melting, forgetfulness-inducing sex. The bed slammed against the wall until it shook so hard she thought it would surely come crashing down on them. Her body had never felt this ravenous, so on fire.

She flew into an orgasm, but he showed no signs of slowing. Nor did her explosive need lessen any when she hurtled over the peak and tumbled down the other side. The bite's influence? They both gasped for breath, their tongues and lips engaged in a duel of intense, thirsty, angry kisses. It didn't matter the cause. She wanted more.

"Again," he growled, echoing her own need.

He held her down and took her deeper. His otherworldly power spilled over her and bound her to him like the ties of invisible restraints. As he thrust, he spoke to her in short, staccato bursts, in a strange language. It might have been curses. Or maybe words of love? There was no way to know because when, between pants, she asked him what he'd said, he just kissed her even harder and touched her in a place that drove the question totally from her mind.

She couldn't think. She could only feel.

So she let go and surrendered to him—to his will to have her and to her own need to belong to this incredible man, heart, soul and body. She let go of her past and gave herself over to an unknown and unfathomable future. And silently prayed that she might spend it with him.

She was getting close again. "Shahin," she pleaded, and his name turned to a breathy moan on her lips. "Come…with me…this time."

"Not yet," he said, and shifted the angle of his entry so the tip of him rubbed against the spot that always sent her into a mindless agony of pleasure.

Again she shattered in his arms, shuddering and quaking as though *she* were his element to call.

Maybe she was.

She gasped out his name and squeezed her eyes shut as her body showed him in vivid detail how much she loved being with him. *How much she loved him…*

Suddenly he slowed his rhythm, and she felt herself being lifted into a sitting position, straddling his lap, his cock still deep inside her. She opened her eyes to see him looking down at her with an expression that sent a stab of raw fear razoring through her. His eyes were shards of ebony, black and hard and glowing with dark intent, his jaw tight and his beautiful mouth curved with secret knowledge.

But of what?

The aftershocks of her orgasm continued to pulse through her, so she wasn't thinking straight. Or she would have remembered immediately what was happening. And understood.

Suddenly, the bed dipped, and a savagely intense male presence slid in behind her. Powerful hands skimmed down her bare arms, leaving a cascade of gooseflesh.

"Seth!" She stiffened instantly recognizing his authoritative touch. How could she have forgotten he'd been there the whole time, watching?

"It's okay, *kalila*. Relax. I'm right here with you," Shahin reassured her, gathering her close.

She knew she'd consented to this, asked for it even, but…oh, God, what was she *doing?*

"Please, I've changed—" she began.

"Shh," Shahin urged brushing a finger across her lips. "Just enjoy the pleasure."

The demigod's energy grew and twined and blended with Shahin's until their erotic magic filled the bed completely, rising like a tide around her, and she was drowning in a sea of irresistible masculine power. It was an overwhelming sensation. Her doubts slipped away under the onslaught of blinding sensual pleasure.

Shahin's arms wrapped around her waist and he easily lifted her, sliding the slick union of their bodies nearly apart, then brought her down again on him, impaling her anew. She moaned and quvered, loving the feel of him inside her.

Then a hot flush of embarrassment flashed through her body, suddenly remembering the other man was right behind her. His excitement and hunger pulsed through her flesh in a formless shock of energy. Not just watching, but touching her.

His hands stroked over her skin and her discomfiture quickly turned to a sizzling heat. Exquisite pleasure spilled down the path where his hands had been. She gave a sharp, breathless moan, and another as Shahin's palms found her breasts and cupped them. He squeezed her nipples and she cried out.

Behind her, she felt Seth's body shift up against her, skin to bare skin. *He'd taken off his clothes.* She sucked in a breath as the hard length of him nestled against her bottom, the ripped muscles of his chest pressed into her back. She felt his warm exhale stir in her hair, mingling with Shahin's, and smelled the sagey scent of his body.

She started to tremble, but was too freaked out to know whether it was from fear or arousal. It felt good. *So* incredibly good. Her body thrilled to be where it was, sandwiched between the two most powerful men she'd ever met.

Then Shahin touched her face and his sex moved inside her, and she again forgot all about the man behind her. Shahin was the man she loved, the only one she wanted. He lifted her and drilled into her, and her flesh responded with a surge of pleasure that left her gasping. *This was nothing like before.* This was—

He did it again. She cried his name. And joined into his movements, together increasing the rhythm to a hard, fast, groaning fever pitch. She felt their mutual climax building, a dull roar rushing toward a full-on gale-force hurricane.

"Now, Gemma, now!" Shahin growled.

She reached for it, closed her eyes and flung herself into the center of the spinning vortex of intense sensation.

And felt the stinging bite of fangs sink into her neck.

She screamed.

Her body detonated. And she was lost down an endless eternity of searing, mind-blowing, exquisite pleasure.

Chapter 19

Shahin felt different when he awoke. More alert. Stronger. Edgier. He was also ravenously hungry.

Gemma stirred, cuddling closer to his side with an exhausted but content sigh. He lifted his head from the pillow and checked on the other side of the bed. Empty. Seth was gone.

Shahin wasn't particularly surprised. The high priest of the God of Darkness was normally awake when it was nighttime aboveground; what little sleep he needed he took during the day. He'd left hours ago to attend to his duties and hadn't returned.

But it hadn't been a dream that Seth had been here last night, in bed with them. There'd been plenty of evidence. Before he'd left, the black satin sheets had been spangled with droplets of red—Gemma's blood—and a larger stain where she'd collapsed after her sacrifice.

It had scared the hell out of Shahin when he'd recovered from their mind-bending sex-and-blood sharing of magic last night and returned to consciousness to find Gemma sprawled under him, unmoving, her neck punctured and streaked by ribbons of blood.

Alarmed, he'd tried to rouse her, but Seth, who'd been lying on the bed next to her with fists clenched, staring fixedly at a point on the ceiling, had ground out, "Let her sleep. She'll be fine."

Shahin had rolled off her and sat up, taking in Seth's rigid posture. "What's wrong? Did something happen?"

Seth slowly unfurled his fists and his muscles, and drew in a deep breath. "No. I'm just having a hard time not taking more from her. Her blood is sweet."

Shahin looked with concern from him to Gemma. "By the gods, Seth, how much did you take?"

"Not much." Seth let out the breath unsteadily. "Not nearly enough. But I want to wait for Josslyn. I need to bind her to me and this is the best way."

Shahin was torn, glad the vampire hadn't taken advantage of Gemma, but also concerned that

Khepesh's leader was growing weaker for every day he went without a full feeding. "I will find the woman before the next moonrise," Shahin vowed, "even if I must bespell Gemma to learn her sister's whereabouts."

"Go gently with her," Seth warned. "Your powers were greatly increased during our sharing and you cannot know the new strength of your magic until it is tested. I advise you to proceed with caution."

Shahin stared at his friend in astonishment. Yet another unexpected thing. "My powers were increased? How?"

Seth eased himself upright and raked his fingers through his hair. "It's part of the exchange. I gain some of your knowledge, you gain some of my power." He glanced over at him. "For obvious reasons, that information is a tightly guarded secret. I'd appreciate if you kept it that way."

"Of course," Shahin said, still shocked. After a pause he asked, "Is that why you haven't shared magic in so many centuries?"

Seth had then given him a half smile. "You always were the most intelligent man on the council. I hope I shall now have advantage of some of that keen intelligence."

Shahin had smiled back at the man he'd served for three-hundred years. "You always have, my lord."

Now, hours later, he glanced over at the woman who'd brought him to this new place of honor among the leaders of Khepesh. As if sensing his regard, Gemma made a contented noise and slid her arm over his midriff, nudging him into a kind of different memory.

She had been amazing last night.

Seth had slipped out of bed just before she woke up for the first time after the blood sacrifice. When she'd opened her eyes, they'd sought first Shahin, who was still sitting on the bed, then looked for Seth. But instead, they had gone big and round when she'd caught sight of the bloodstained bed linens. Her hand flew to her neck and came away sticky red.

"Am I— Did he—"

"You're fine," Shahin assured her. "It looks much worse than it was. Would you like to clean up?"

She nodded, and they indulged in his luxurious two-headed shower. Afterward, he dried her, then carefully bandaged her twin wounds. But not before they'd explored the lingering physical power of the bite marks. He wondered how long the erotic effect would last.

As they nestled down under fresh, clean sheets, he cocked his head at her, curious. "How do you feel?"

Her tongue swiped over her lip and her gaze

dipped to his nude body. "Like I just had a three-day-long orgasm…and could go for another three. Years."

With a lascivious smile, he crawled over her on all fours. "I believe that could be arranged."

They made love again. And again. And again. He lost count of the number of times. Apparently one of the heightened powers he'd acquired from the exchange of magic was the vampire's inexhaustible sexual prowess. And it was better than it had ever been before.

Gemma had been pleased. Endlessly.

Watching her now as she slept, he wondered if she'd been bonded to him through the ritual. Earlier, he'd wanted it to happen; but now, outside the heat of the moment, he wasn't sure it would be such a good thing after all. He wanted Gemma's adoration, yes. And her love and her unfailing loyalty. But he wanted it honestly. Because of her true feelings for him. Not as the result of a spell—or a curse, depending on one's perspective on the matter.

Well, it was too late now. What would be was already written. There was no changing one's fate.

"Shahin?" she murmured, her eyelids fluttering open.

"Yes, *kalila?*"

Her lips curved as she snuggled closer to his

body. She gazed up at him with soft, trusting eyes and whispered, "I love you."

His heart stilled. And an odd little ache began in it. He gave her forehead a lingering kiss and said, "I'm very glad."

I'm very glad.

Wow. Okay, so maybe that was just about the response Gemma had expected of Shahin.

But definitely not the one she'd wanted to hear.

Honestly? If the man didn't have feelings for her after the last two nights, she figured it was never going to happen. She herself had fallen completely, utterly and irrevocably in love with the recalcitrant sheikh. Probably at first sight. The past two days and nights had only intensified her feelings.

Damn.

She stifled a sigh. She would *not* be upset.

After all, she'd have all eternity to work on him.

The thought cheered her.

Somewhat.

"Gemma," he said.

"Yes?"

"Will you tell us now where your sister is?"

The cheer froze in her chest. Hurt spiraled through her.

Had all this been staged—the banquet, the bite,

the fabulous sex—just to get her to tell them what they wanted to know?

Of course it had. Seth-Aziz had made no secret of his intentions with this ritual—to get to Josslyn. Shahin's reasons were murkier. Okay, make that simpler. Great sex was a perfectly normal goal in itself, for a man. He'd said so himself. Plus he was just doing his job—again, to get Joss. He'd also told her that.

Little did he realize that she had already decided to find her sister and tell her everything.

"I honestly don't know where she is," she told Shahin, quietly resigned to her unrequited feelings. "But yes, I'll help you."

For a second, he didn't move. Then he shifted onto his side and slid his body up to hers. "You will?"

She nodded. "You were right. It's her life. Josslyn should make her own decision."

He gazed over at her happily. "That's good." But his smile faded. "What is it, Gemma?"

She blinked. Realized her thoughts must be showing. She forced a smile to her lips. "Nothing. Why?"

"You look almost…sad."

"No. Just tired." She reached out and brushed her fingers over his chest. He was still nude and so handsome that it made her heart ache. Or perhaps that was something else... "We haven't gotten much sleep the past couple of days," she added when he still looked doubtful.

His breath soughed over her, warm and easy, as his smile returned. "Sleep, then, *kalila*. I'll be here when you wake, and we can go find Josslyn together."

He kissed her, and she turned to her side, giving him her back. She was afraid if she faced him she wouldn't be able to keep the bleakness from her eyes. He scooted close and spooned her body with his. It felt so good, so right, to be with him like this, their naked, sated bodies sharing a peaceful slumber.

So good it almost made her forget that it wasn't real. That Shahin's warmth and the magic of his love were all part of a beautiful illusion. Just a brief desert fantasy.

Shahin couldn't sleep.

He didn't know what to do about Gemma. *She'd said she loved him.* Out of the blue. What further proof did he need that the bonding had, indeed, taken place?

He felt sick. He'd had no right to do this to her, to take her choice away.

He waited until her body relaxed and her breathing was even, then he slipped out of bed, got dressed and grabbed his scimitar. As he made his

way through the corridors of Khepesh to the armory
on the other side of the palace, he could still smell
the scent of her on his skin. He could almost feel
the curve of her body nestled against his.

Sekhmet's blood, he missed her already.

When he got to the armory, he called to one of
the guards lounging in the great practice hall to
come cross swords with him. He badly needed to
bash someone.

Most of his men had been at the banquet and seen
him with Gemma. The bare chest display. The kiss.
The possessive scowl on his face whenever another
man approached.

"Has the lady kicked you from her bed already,
my lord?" one of them quipped from across the
hall.

"On the contrary," Shahin shot back. "She sleeps
from exhaustion!"

The men laughed and gathered to watch as he
and his opponent chose their weapons and took their
stances. At a signal from his second-in-command,
they raised their swords and lunged. In one stroke,
Shahin had disarmed the other man and felled him
to the floor with a crash. Surprise rippled through
the onlookers. And him as well. Shahin was good,
better than any other warrior in the land, but it
usually took more than a single blow, even for him,
to win a match.

"My lord," his lieutenant exclaimed into the somewhat stunned silence, "whatever this new woman has done to you tonight, you must share her secret!"

Shahin stared down at the sword in his hands. He cleared his throat. "No secret. It must be the adrenaline that still flows from our bedplay."

His men snorted in amusement, but didn't question the explanation, though in his mind, Shahin did. Was this what Seth meant about increased powers?

"Be sure to tell us when you've tired of her, my lord," called another above the bawdy comments. "So we may all avail ourselves of her warrior magic!"

Shahin sent the man a stony look. "Another man may have her when I am dead."

A wave of raised eyebrows went through the men. But before any dared respond, a messenger came running into the armory. "Sheikh Shahin!" he shouted. "The war! It's starting, my lord! A troop of Haru-Re's men have breached the borderlands and are riding hard for Khepesh!"

Chapter 20

"Gem."

A woman's hushed voice drew Gemma out of a deep, drugging sleep. It sounded wonderfully familiar.

"Gemma!" This time it was accompanied by a gentle shake. "Wake up!"

She pried her eyelids open. And couldn't believe her eyes. "Gillian!" She rocketed upright and instantly regretted it. Her head spun so badly that she fell back to the bed again. "What— How— Oh, my God, is it really you?" She rubbed her eyes in disbelief.

Gillian reached out and took her hands. "Yes, it's really me. But we must talk quickly."

Gemma frowned as the image of her sister flickered. The solid feel of her hands did the same, suddenly gone, then back again, as though some cosmic matter-antimatter toggle switch had been thrown. She shook her head to clear it, certain it was her own brain misfiring. "I don't understand. What's going on?"

"I'm really here," Gillian said in a rush, "but you're dreaming me, through a magic spell. An ancient one that Haru-Re found and is using against Khepesh. You have to warn Seth-Aziz."

Gemma sucked down another breath and took a second shot at sitting up. This time her head didn't spin like a top, thank God. She needed all her faculties to figure out what the hell Gillian was talking about. "Slow down, Jelly Bean. "I don't understand."

Gillian pulled a small parchment scroll from her pocket and placed it in Gemma's hand. "Give this to Nephtys. It's a copy of the spell. I'm using it now, but only with Rhys's help. It takes a lot of power and I don't know how long he can keep it up."

Gemma nodded and set the scroll aside, along with the shock that her sister was using magic. "My God, Gillian, are you all right? Shahin told me you and Rhys are—" She stopped abruptly, unwilling to repeat the harsh accusation. "That you've joined Haru-Re at Petru. Is that true?"

Gillian started to shake her head. "It's complic—" Suddenly, she stopped and glanced around, taking in the room. Her gaze stalled on the rumpled sheets and dented pillows, then the masculine accoutrements and the captain of the guard's distinctive emblems. Her eyes widened. "Wait. Where are you, Gemma?" she asked, aghast. "Is this *Shahin's* bed?"

"Come back to Khepesh," Gemma urged, ignoring her sister's dismayed question. "Seth-Aziz forgives you and Rhys for running away. He's—he's now convinced that Joss is the one meant to be his consort."

Gillian's jaw dropped. "And you're *okay* with tha—" All at once her sister spotted the bandage on Gemma's neck and gasped. "Oh, my freaking *lord*, Gemma! You didn't!"

Gemma blinked, reached up to touch the bandage on her neck, and battled back a wave of erotic sensation. She volleyed her little sister's words back at her. "It's complicated, Jelly Bean. But please, you've got to come back to Khepesh. They're talking about war with Haru-Re, and I couldn't bear if anything—"

"I can't, Gem," Gillian interrupted, and grabbed Gemma's hands, her eyes growing serious. Again her image flickered for a few suspenseful seconds. Then she said, "I can't leave Mom and Dad."

A wall of shock hit Gemma, knocking her back as though she'd been shot. "Mom and Dad?"

Seth was *right*. Her mother was a captive of Haru-Re in *Petru!*

But…

"Dad?" Gemma asked, her eyes welling with tears. *"Dad* is alive? He's there, too?"

Gillian nodded as her eyes filled. "He's good. He's living here as one of Ray's immortals. He'd figured out what happened to Mom and wanted to be with her. That's why he left us. She's…not herself."

Tears trickled down Gemma's cheeks as she realized what her sister was saying. She'd occasionally seen the silent, unobtrusive servants called *shabti*. The ones Shahin had told her had been robbed of their will and personality when they'd gotten too close to learning the secrets of Set-Sutekh's tomb-palace, but had for whatever reason refused to become an initiate. They seemed healthy and serene and were well treated—at least here in Khepesh. But the thought of their endless, vacant lives had broken Gemma's heart.

And now her own mother—*Oh, God*.

Gillian's arms came around her and they held each other tight and let their bittersweet tears fall; tears of sadness for their mother's fate, and tears of joy that their father still lived.

"Find Josslyn and come to Petru," Gillian begged through her sniffles. She pulled away a little and gave Gemma a pleading look. "We can all be together here. Bring Shahin if you can't live without him. He can be a spy for Khepesh, like Rhys."

A warring riot of feelings surged through Gemma. How could she betray Khepesh? She'd only been here for a day, but already it felt like home. And what about Seth and Nephtys? It would feel like stabbing them in the back. And as for Shahin... He would never, ever consent to defect to Petru. Not in a billion years.

But how could she *not* go and be reunited? They were her parents! Her *family!*

"Oh, Gillian, I—"

But suddenly, Gillian was gone. Vanished. Cold emptiness filled Gemma's arms in place of the warm comfort of her sister's hug.

"Gillian!" Gemma called out in dismay. She jumped up from the bed and twirled around in a circle, searching desperately around the room. But there was no sign of her. *"No!"*

* * *

It was nearly sunrise.

Shahin and his men found the troop of enemy warriors ten miles inside Khepesh's borders. They were riding like wildfire, dozens of them, pouring over the desert sands like a cloud of yellow locusts. Their golden armor flashed in the bleeding light of dawn, the hides of their camels ceremonially gilded with the distinctive signs and glyphs of their god, Re-Horakhti, God of the Sun and Lord of the Horizon.

Shahin let out an oath. *By Sekhmet's claw*, there were a lot of them. His own troop was only ten warriors, the men who'd been in the armory, minus his lieutenant who'd stayed to rouse the rest of the guard to action.

This could get ugly.

No, this *would* get ugly. There was no way they would win against such odds.

Time for the ultimate sacrifice.

He grimly gave a signal to his runner to fly back to Khepesh with orders for his lieutenant to lock down the palace and go to full battle stations. When he and his men fell, he didn't want Haru-Re getting past the gates.

Their sacrifice would *not* be in vain.

"Switch mounts!" he ordered the troop. As

242 Shadow of the Sheikh

one, their ghost camels morphed into huge black war stallions, pawing the air and snorting with excitement. The beasts could smell the coming battle.

Shahin could, too. The smell that permeated the desert air was sharp and tingly in his nostrils, a heady blend of power and ancient magic. The heat of it slithered along his arms like the rub of snakeskin.

He frowned, narrowing his eyes. He'd never been able to smell magic before. Sense it? Yes. But this was a discernible tang being carried on the breeze. Another of Seth's vampyric gifts?

Or a new, sinister spell cast by Haru-Re?

He would soon find out.

He drew his scimitar. "Praise be to God!" he shouted, raising his weapon above his head. "We fight!"

"For the glory of Set-Sutekh!" the men shouted back, drawing steel.

At the last second, an image of Gemma filled Shahin's mind. What a shame that he must die on the very day realized he loved her and wanted her for all time.

Still, he'd been lucky to have won her love at all—this woman who'd given herself to him so fully and freely. These past two precious days with

Gemma had been worth more than ten times ten-thousand days without her.

With a heart filled with the strength gained of the knowledge of love, he gave the order.

"To the death!"

His men let out an answering yell. The massive horses reared.

And they charged into the fray.

Chapter 21

Nephtys hurried to her meditation room and almost threw herself down on her knees in front of the Eye of Horus, her scrying bowl. All Khepesh was abuzz with the news of Haru-Re's impending attack. But Seth had locked her in her rooms with a triple guard posted at her door. No one was allowed in or out.

She needed to know what was happening!

Lord Shahin had ridden out to try and head off the invaders, but if the frantic report of his messenger was even remotely accurate, the small troop of guards didn't stand much of a chance.

She felt a wrenching stab of guilt and remorse for the sheikh's certain loss. He was a good friend and there was no one in all of Khepesh more loyal to her brother. Shahin's death would be on *her* head. The war might not be her fault, but this battle surely was.

How she cursed her knowledge of the magic of immortality! She wished to the goddess she'd never become a priestess. That decision had brought nothing but grief into her life. She would have been better off staying a slave!

With shaking hands she fetched the holy water and poured it into the golden bowl, spilling half. Anxiously she sat and awaited the vision that would appear. And waited.

"Come on!" she cried, wringing her hands.

Finally, the surface of the water rippled softly and the clear blue slowly started to cloud.

Too slowly!

She wanted to shout with impatience as it darkened to cobalt and hovered there in shadowed obscurity.

"Please!" she begged.

She needed to see an image of the desert above! She needed to see men fighting! She needed to watch Set-Sutekh bring forth a miracle so Shahin and his men could claim a glorious victory over impossible odds!

Instead, the bowl remained frustratingly, maddeningly cloaked in a veil of indigo.

Except… What was that?

In the depths of the seemingly blank vision, something moved. And she realized there was an image. Dim, indistinct, nearly impossible to make out, but there it was! *A bed.*

She blinked several times and leaned in. Yes, it was a bed. In a darkened room. And there was a figure in it. That's what had moved.

The figure moved again. It resolved itself into a woman's form. Nephtys peered closer.

The woman looked like Gillian Haliday! But…a bit older. Was she seeing the future, perhaps?

No! This must be *Josslyn* Haliday! Shahin had said she looked just like her sister.

Then, something else moved in the vision. Behind the bed. Something that—

Sweet Isis!

Nephtys's gasp echoed sharply through the meditation chamber. There were three men standing next to Josslyn's bed, arms folded across their brawny chests, as though guarding the sleeping woman. But Nephtys knew better.

They were Haru-Re's men.

"Well, that's convenient," the voice of the man himself said from right behind her. "I was afraid you wouldn't believe me."

She leaped to her feet on another gasp and landed

in his iron grip. He seized her arms and held her fast. "Let me go!" she cried. "Or I'll scream!"

"Go ahead," he said. "No one will hear you. This is a dream, remember?"

She tried to pull away, but it was no use. "I'm not asleep!" At least…she didn't think so.

He smiled and brushed a finger down her cheek. Sparks followed the movement. "Perhaps not. The spell is working its magic, blurring your lines between sleep and waking. Soon I may come to you anytime I wish and you'll be powerless to stop me."

She shivered. "You're wrong, Haru-Re. I'll find a ward against you if it's the last thing I do."

His smile just widened. "Good luck with that." He glanced over her shoulder at the vision still playing out in the scrying bowl. "Meanwhile, my sweet, I shall have another amusement with which to divert myself."

"Don't you *dare!*" She jerked away from him and this time she succeeded. "I'm telling you, leave Josslyn Haliday alone!"

His elegant black brows rose. "Or what?"

She wanted to slap him for his insolence and his accursed arrogance. It wouldn't have given her an answer to his infuriating question, but it would have felt oh, so very gratifying.

"I thought not," he said smugly. He waved a hand

over the vision. The men looked up at him, and he ordered them, "Bring the woman to Petru."

"No!" Nephtys cried as they stepped toward the sleeping mortal. "Wait!"

Haru-Re raised a hand for the men to halt. Then he leveled a look at Nephtys. The air around him shimmered. "I'm listening."

Isis give her strength! If Haru-Re took Josslyn, Seth would be devastated. He had never obsessed over a new consort before, not like he was with this one. It was as though her brother instinctively knew that Josslyn Haliday represented the last good hope for the future of Khepesh and their god. He'd trusted Nephtys's vision of this mortal woman's wisdom and, she suspected, he yearned for the glimpse of true love it hinted at.

Nephtys couldn't let the enemy defeat their beloved god. Or worse, steal her brother's eternal happiness.

She just *couldn't*. She would rather die a slow death herself.

Therefore, she knew what she must do.

"What do you want for her freedom?" she asked.

"You know my price," he said, his eyes glittering with imminent conquest.

She swallowed heavily, knowing only too well who would be the vanquished. "Me. My services are to be shared between Khepesh and Petru for five hundred years. I believe that was the bargain you offered Lord Kilpatrick last week." She nearly choked on the words.

Haru-Re laughed. "I'm afraid that offer has run out. Rhys Kilpatrick is now one of mine. And this hostage—" he pointed at Josslyn "—is worth far more than five hundred years of sharing you."

Her stomach sank. "How long then? Six hundred?"

Sparks flew. He gave her a withering look. "Please, you insult me."

"Eight hundred? A thousand?" she asked with growing apprehension.

"There will be no sharing!" he boomed angrily. Above him, a bust of fireworks showered down, sending hot pinpricks over her skin. Then he took a calming breath and said, "It is only fair that Seth-Aziz and I make an even trade. Don't you think?"

She froze in consternation, suddenly terrified, foreboding exploding within her as surely as his fireworks. "What do you mean an even trade?"

He grasped her chin and lifted it so she must look him in his devilish eyes. "I mean, my love," he growled, his voice low and thick with triumph, "if Seth-Aziz wishes to have this Haliday woman as his consort, then you must become mine!"

Chapter 22

Shahin's scimitar sliced through the neck of an enemy warrior, abruptly cutting off the man's scream. Crimson blood spurted into the sky like a fountain.

Hell, this one, at least, had died.

Thank the gods!

Shahin calmed his rearing mount and prepared himself for the next vicious attack. His troop of Khepesh guards were fighting fiercely, but so far, Shahin was the only one who'd scored a kill.

What in the name of Sekhmet's teat was going on?

From the corner of his eyes, he watched the

swords of his men cut and parry, only to pass through their opponents as though they were made of air.

With a start, Shahin suddenly understood. They were fighting apparitions! Conjured wisps of illusion—much like their own mounts.

Another bore down on him with a savage sneer, weapon poised to part Shahin's head from his body, He slashed out with his scimitar, to no avail. He ducked and wheeled out of the way. *Sweet Osiris.* If not a blade, what in God's name would kill the bastards?

The answer came swiftly, and just in time to save the man fighting next to him. A ghost warrior charged full bore, golden sword flying over his head in a deadly swirl. Shahin focused, gathering the powers within him into a giant, quaking, thundering ball of energy. He flung it hard at the enemy.

It struck with the slamming *boom* of an earthquake. The warrior's body splintered like a broken mirror, shattered bits of power flung outward in a glittering rainbow of dying pulses.

The Khepesh man he'd saved let out a triumphant yell. "My lord! You killed it!"

Shahin wheeled his mount, scanning the battlefield. *Good God.* One down, dozens to go.

"Guards of Set-Sutekh!" he shouted. "Use your

magic! They are but phantoms. Shatter them if you can, keep them busy if you can't!"

Instantly, his men regrouped and followed his orders. They fought like devils. But despite their considerable magical abilities, his guards were powerless against the enemy horde.

So it was all up to Shahin.

It took every ounce of his powerful magic to overcome the never-ending river of tenacious fighting phantoms, worked on horseback and at the last second before being sliced to ribbons himself. He was certain it was only thanks to his enhanced powers from last night's exchange with Seth that he had the ability to eventually turn the tide, one by one.

When it was over, Shahin reined in his horse, scraped the blood from his brow with his sleeve and shaded his eyes against the blazing morning sun. He did a full-circle, quickly searching the battlefield for any movement. There was none.

They had earned their legendary moniker today: the death warriors of Set-Sutekh had triumphed once again.

Not one of the enemy had been left alive. And yet, for the amount of killing he and his men had done, surprisingly few bodies littered the ground. Of the entire horde of invaders only a handful had been flesh-and-blood immortals, and those few now lay sprawled on the sand minus their heads, well and truly dead.

Shahin scowled and studied the remains as he regained his breath and slowed his heartbeat from the fury of battle.

A bad feeling climbed up his spine like an arachnid.

Something was not right about this.

The enemy had put on a good show, but not good enough. Ten men had won against five score?

"My lord! Victory is ours!" one of his men shouted jubilantly as the others rode up to join him with a clatter of hooves.

Shahin narrowed his eyes and continued to stare at the battlefield.

"My lord? Something wrong? Are you injured?"

He turned to meet their concerned gazes. "Believe me, no one is happier than I to be alive. But this was far too easy a victory for us."

His men stirred on their mounts, frowning. "Sir? If it hadn't been for your powers, we could never have prevailed."

True enough. Still… "If this is an invasion, where are the rest of Petru's immortal guard? It's like this conjured force was sent just to test us, win or lose," Shahin mused.

"That makes no sense," another man said,

sheathing his bloody sword. "Why would Haru-Re send even a handful of his men to die for no reason?"

"Men he can ill-afford to sacrifice," a third reminded him. "He has more immortals than we, but his numbers are dwindling because Petru has no priestess to create new ones. We do. Our loss could be made up for. Not these men." He pointed to the dead.

"Indeed," Shahin said grimly. Then comprehension hit him like a blade in the gut. He should have seen it sooner. *Nephtys.* The priestess had long been the object of Haru-Re's stratagems. This battle was surely a diversion, to lure him and the palace guards away from Khepesh to make a bid for her capture.

It was a damn good thing he'd decided to leave the bulk of the guard minding the palace. His troop's willing sacrifice had paid off.

An errant thought of Gemma flashed through his mind. Perhaps he wasn't meant to die today after all.

He wheeled his mount and shouted the order, "Gentlemen, shift! We must return to Khepesh with all haste!"

With a whirl of robes, a flash of wings and fur and a slow dissolve of their mounts, he and his men shifted to their Set-animal forms and flew, pounded and scampered toward the palace.

Shahin just prayed they would get there in time to help save their home and loved ones.

When the small troop arrived at the Great Western Gate, everything seemed…completely normal.

The bulk of the guard ran out to greet them as the gate swung open to admit the ragged and bloody warriors. No one had expected to see them again. At least not alive. "By Thot's scales, it's good to greet you, my lord!" his lieutenant called heartily. "Hail to the conquering heroes!" There were cheers and slaps on the back as the valiant troop entered.

Shahin quickly pulled his lieutenant aside with a wary frown. "Is all well here at the palace, then?"

"Yes, my lord. Every one of the guard is on duty, full alert and battle stations as ordered. All has been quiet."

Shahin was fairly stunned. So the battle *hadn't* been a diversion? "Seth-Aziz? The Lady Nephtys?"

"Both safe. Lord Seth is in his audience chamber, the priestess locked safely in her rooms. Guards are posted at both doors."

"And outside, at the old tomb entrance?" he pressed. As they'd found out the night Rhys Kilpatrick and Lady Gillian escaped Khepesh, the only other way out of the palace was through a hidden door in the council chamber which led to Seth-Aziz's ancient tomb. Few knew about the secret tomb entrance, but it was the palace's spot of greatest vulnerability. Now it was always guarded.

"Ten men, and guards posted every ten feet along the tunnel," the lieutenant confirmed. "As ordered."

Shahin nodded, mystified, but satisfied that Khepesh was not under attack. "Good. Keep the outer guard on full alert and the inside guard doubled, but the others can stand down for now. And see that today's victors are well rewarded for their efforts. I'll be with the high priest."

"Yes, my lord."

Shahin made his way to the audience chamber where he found Seth pacing back and forth, awaiting word from him. After his report, Seth was equally suspicious, but neither could come up with an explanation for Haru-Re's actions.

"I'm still uneasy about this," Shahin said. "I want to find Josslyn Haliday and fetch her here to Khepesh immediately." Could Haru-Re have somehow found out about Josslyn and the diversion was aimed at capturing her, and not Nephtys?

Seth nodded somberly. "I only hope you're not too late. One can't help but think the timing is too close to be a coincidence."

Shahin looked down at himself, still covered with the filth of battle. "With your permission I'll clean up first, then take Gemma and go."

Seth waved his hand to urge him away. "Make haste. Send word the minute you have her."

"I will."

Assuming Haru-Re hadn't found her first.

Where *was* the man?

Gemma had awoken to an empty bed and an empty apartment. Shahin had *promised* to be there when she awoke. But once again, she'd reached for him and he'd been gone.

Seth had also been gone. That, however, was a relief. The things he'd seen her and Shahin do in bed last night, she didn't think she could ever look the demigod in the eye again. Or herself in the mirror, for that matter. Every time she spotted the neat white bandage on her neck, she nearly died of mortification. She'd let herself be bitten by a vampire! And sweet mercy, how she and Shahin had enjoyed it…

Gemma's mind was in chaos. Between his being gone, the vampire bite on her neck and that weird dream last night when Gillian had come to her with news of their parents being alive in Petru, she was totally freaked out.

Even more so when she found the parchment scroll lying on the bed. Good God, it *hadn't* been a dream? Gillian had actually been there! The dream-spell parchment she'd left Gemma to give to Nephtys was proof! If *that* was real, it meant the part about her parents must also be real.

Her mother and father were alive! At Petru. And Gillian wanted her to leave Khepesh to be with them.

Gemma was so confused. She needed to talk to Shahin about this. Or at least to Nephtys.

But the guards at the apartment door would not let her leave. It didn't matter that she only wanted to visit the priestess. They had their orders directly from their captain and they would not disobey.

When she asked in frustration about Shahin, where he was, their gazes slid away almost guiltily and they refused to tell her. Why? Was *he* in some kind of danger?

Of course he was. He was a warrior, captain of the palace guard. His whole life was about danger.

God save him.

And her.

So when he finally strode through the door, she jumped up and launched herself into his arms. "Thank God! Oh, Shahin, where have you been? What's going on? I've been so worried!" Her anxious words poured out in a flood until his surprise finally turned to laughter and he hugged and kissed her to shut her up.

"I'm fine," he said as she covered his gritty face in kisses. "But filthy. Help me get undressed. I need a shower."

She banked her eagerness to talk and gladly obliged. She joined him under the water. "I missed you," she murmured. Holding him in her arms, she realized how true it was. She'd missed him terribly from the second she'd awakened to find him gone. How could she ever think about going to Petru without him?

After he washed, they made love under the cascading water. It felt different than it had before. Closer, somehow. Shahin felt more vulnerable. More emotional. And a bit more desperate.

"What is it, Shahin?" she asked when they were melting in each other's arms, wrapped in the afterglow of their lovemaking.

Water ran down their bodies in warm rivulets as his silence stretched, broken only by the hiss and patter of the spray. Spice-scented steam swirled about them, turning the glass stall into a private cocoon.

Shahin pushed out a breath and tightened his embrace. At length he said, "Nothing. I'm just so damn glad to be here with you. I don't ever want to move from this place."

She gazed up at him, the worry beginning to

trickle back. "Did something happen while you were out?"

He shook his head. She wasn't convinced. But she was outright shocked when he began, "Gemma, last night you said you love me. Was that—"

But he never got to complete the question. It was drowned out by a sudden frantic pounding on the apartment door.

"My lord!" someone yelled. "Sheikh Shahin! You're needed immediately! The lady Nephtys. She's been taken captive!"

Gemma hurried down the main palace corridor after Shahin, a clutch of guards close at their heels. He'd given orders they weren't to leave her sight. They were all headed for the council chamber, where Seth-Aziz awaited.

She didn't know what was going on and was frightened out of her wits. How could the priestess have been snatched out from the hidden depths of an underground palace? It didn't seem possible.

Shahin apparently shared her opinion. That was the first question he asked of Seth when they swept into the chamber.

The high priest sat at the end of a long obsidian conference table, leaning on his elbows, his head in his hands, obviously in distress.

When they entered, he looked up. "She's surrendered to him, Shahin! Nephtys has sacrificed herself to that bastard!" He rose to his feet, fists pounding the table.

Gemma shrank back against the stone wall of the chamber, trying to make herself as small as possible against the demigod's rage. Her guards hung back in the doorway.

Shahin's stopped in his tracks, obviously shocked. "Why in the name of Osiris would she do that?"

Seth pushed a parchment note across the table. "Read for yourself!" he thundered.

Shahin scanned the parchment, then glanced at Gemma with a scowl and back to Seth. "She *traded* herself for Josslyn?" he said in visible disbelief.

Gemma jumped to attention. *What?*

Seth drilled his fingers into his hair. "It's over, Shahin! My own sister has doomed Khepesh to extinction!"

But what about *her* sister?

"That's not necessarily true," Shahin said to Seth, trying to calm the high priest's agitation. He swiped a hand over his lower face, rubbing his jaw. "If Lady Nephtys did this, she must have good reason. And a plan. She loves you, Seth, and Khepesh as well. She would never put us in danger. She'd rather die than betray you. You know that."

Seth's eyes squeezed shut. "Until ten minutes ago, I would have staked my life on that being true." He opened them again and jetted out a breath. "Now it appears I *have* staked my life upon it."

Gemma peered back and forth between the men. "What about Josslyn?" she blurted out, unable to contain her fears any longer. "Is *she* in danger?"

Seth's mouth pressed into a thin, angry line. "Only if she is unlucky enough to cross my path," he ground out.

"Nephtys says Haru-Re has sworn to leave her alone," Shahin assured her.

Alarm zinged through Gemma's insides. "And you *believe* him?" She turned to Seth. "S-sir, my lord," she faltered, "I th-thought you wanted her here, to be your—"

Seth slashed a hand down like a hatchet, cutting her off. "I never want to see her face! Or hear her name spoken before me again! This is all *her* fault! If it weren't for her—"

Gemma gasped. "That's unfair!" she cried as Shahin sent her a warning glance, shaking his head. Gemma ignored him. "Josslyn didn't have anything to do with your decision to—"

"Enough!" Seth boomed and took a step toward her. "Have a care, girl, or you, too, will be banished from my sight!"

Shahin stepped in front of her protectively. "My lord, I'll take Gemma with me to the oasis encampment and contact my spies to dig up what they can about Nephtys's situation at Petru."

"Yes," Seth snapped. "Do that! I want to know if she really intends to go through with this madness. My sister, Haru-Re's *consort*! It is an abomination!" The normally stoic demigod's voice pitched to a roar.

Gemma tugged on the back of Shahin's tunic. "Josslyn?" she whispered urgently, unable to get past him to ask Seth herself.

Shahin cursed under his breath, and asked, "And the Haliday woman, my lord?"

"You heard me. I want nothing to do with the troublemaker! Haru-Re has promised her safety. Leave her to her mortal fate. Now *go*."

She and Shahin exited the council chamber quickly. Once in the hall, with the door closed, Gemma reached for Shahin and clung to him with shaking hands. "He didn't really mean that, did he?"

"I don't know," Shahin admitted. "But for now, I think it's best we leave Josslyn where she is."

Gemma was terrified for her sister, being out there all on her own to face whatever otherworldly machinations were working around her. It was obvious Haru-Re knew about Joss and was using her to his own ends. Could they really trust his promise?

If he realized Joss had been abandoned by Seth, what would he do to her then?

Josslyn needed to be here, at Khepesh, safe and protected.

And the irony of *that* complete reversal in her attitude did not escape Gemma.

But then she remembered Gillian's plea.

Maybe she and Joss really did belong at Petru, to be with Gillian and their mother and father. If they gave themselves up to Haru-Re, maybe he would honor the trade and let Nephtys go. That way Seth could be happy again.

But…what about Shahin? What would she do without him?

God, what a mess.

How could she even *think* about leaving the man she loved?

Chapter 23

Nephtys could see the dazzling blaze of Haru-Re's anger even before he entered the temple. A living thing, the light of his fury filled the sky above Petru like a thousand suns, flashing, glittering, bright enough to blind.

Nephtys gathered her strength, calling forth every vestige of power she possessed. She would need every ounce of it to face him down.

The demigod did not like to be crossed. She would feel his wrath. But she was ready to bear it.

For Khepesh. For her brother.

"Priestess!" he bellowed, storming into the temple sanctuary like a tornado of shimmering radiance. Tall, broad, handsome and as golden as the sun he worshipped, his sculpted features were chiseled in a mask of determination.

By the goddess, he was magnificent!

"Yes, my lord?" she answered softly. She did not rise from where she knelt at her prayers before the altar of Re-Horakhti, but she did look up. Temple acolytes scattered like seeds in a storm.

He towered above her, his long fingers curled into tight fists. Sparks exploded around him in a living halo. "You dare break your sacred oath to a demigod?" he roared.

"No, my lord," she refuted calmly, though her knees were trembling. "I have not broken my word."

He raged on as though she had not spoken. "You shall become my consort immediately! That was our agreement!"

Now she did rise. Slowly and with the dignity befitting her high rank. Not easy with a huge devil looming over her and pricks of fire raining down on her bare skin.

"No," she said. "I agreed to become your consort, but nothing was said about when."

A glower swept across his patrician features. "You know damned well—"

"I am a priestess, my lord," she interrupted, though her heart quailed, "and I must discharge those duties before taking up those as your wife. It takes time for the rituals."

"A *year?*" he growled furiously. "You seek to provoke me!"

"What is one more year compared to the five-thousand you have lived quite happily without me?"

He seized her arms and glared down at her, but the rain of embers diminished. "You keep bringing that up. You must have missed me greatly to be so nettled by my absence."

She felt her cheeks go warm. "Like a slave misses the master who sold her."

"I never sold you," he said, his eyes narrowing dangerously. "You were stolen from me."

According to whose version of the story?

"It matters not. I am no longer a slave, and you must respect the ways of the temple or lose the favor of your god," she reminded him. "Will you not need the help of Re-Horakhti in the coming battle against my brother and Khepesh?"

She watched him mentally weigh the risks of defying the god he served. Ray had always done exactly as he wished, but always within the laws of Petru. Not that there was an actual law concerning the obscure ritual she was invoking. But he didn't need to know that.

"Do not think," he said, his voice low and rough, "that you will escape my bed for a year, *meruati*."

My only heart. She hated when he called her that. It weakened her will to hold him at bay. And it wasn't true. He *had* no heart. Yet her pulse sped whenever he whispered the endearment.

He pulled her body close to his. His lips sought hers.

Her heart beat out of control. At the last second, she turned her cheek. "We have no choice. I must stay pure for the ritual."

She prayed fervently he wouldn't question the lie.

Against her throat she felt the erotic scrape of his fangs as they lengthened. She shivered, and tried to pull away from him.

He held her firm, with arms of unbreakable granite. "We shall see," he murmured, and glided the tip of his tongue perilously close to the nearly faded bite with which he'd marked her. Her addiction from him flared to a burn. Her body clenched with need.

"No," she whispered.

"You are mine, Nephtys," he purred into her ear. "Your blood, your body, your soul. *Mine.* And no one will ever take you away from me again. *No one.*"

Chapter 24

"Shahin, there's something I need to tell you."

The anxious way Gemma said those words made Shahin halt as he reached for her. She looked troubled.

This could not be good.

She was pacing back and forth across his tent—*their* tent—wearing a path in the Persian rug. She was still incredibly upset about Seth's pronouncement regarding Josslyn. They'd returned to the oasis this morning when it had become apparent there was nothing to be done to change his mind. Not at this point, anyway.

Shahin watched her continue to pace. Now what?

There was no way of predicting what she was about to spring on him. He was as much at a loss today to decipher her thoughts as he'd been since the first moment he saw her. If there was one thing he'd learned about Gemma Haliday, it was that she never did or said what was expected.

"Oh?" he prompted, dread circling his insides like a starving jackal.

She stopped pacing but wouldn't meet his gaze. "I saw Gillian last night."

He frowned. "What?"

"While you were gone."

His body stilled. But confusion jumbled his mind. "That's impossible. Gillian is at Petru."

To his further confusion, she nodded. "Yeah."

She finally turned to face him. "I don't really understand it, but…she came to me, to Khepesh, while I was sleeping."

Relief surged through him. *Ptah's feather.* For a minute there… "In a dream, you mean," he clarified.

She shook her head. "No. It wasn't a dream. She was there with me. In your bedroom. Sort of. She said it was a spell. Rhys Kilpatrick was helping her work it. Like I said, I didn't really get the details. I just know she was there, talking to me. It was weird. She flickered. Like an old movie, badly spliced."

He narrowed his eyes. Digested that. "I've

never heard of a spell like that." It was possible one existed, he supposed. If true, it would be a formidable weapon in the *per netjer*'s arsenal. Maybe Seth had kept it a secret, like he'd kept the powers of sharing magic under wraps.

Gemma dashed that notion. "Gillian said Haru-Re recently rediscovered it. That he'd been using it on Nephtys. That's how he got to her. To threaten."

Ah. That made more sense. But the question occurred to him, perhaps a tad cynically... How had Gillian gotten hold of it so easily? "Does Seth know about this spell?" he asked.

"I'm not sure. She was only here for a few minutes and we talked about...other things." She folded her arms over her abdomen, looking ill.

Apprehension tingled over his scalp. "What things? What did she want?" he asked, his uneasiness increasing tenfold. He had a feeling he wasn't going to like the answer.

Gemma bit her lip, and blurted out, "She told me my parents are alive. Both of them. living at Petru."

Shahin's insides went cold as ice. He knew about the mother, of course. But the father, too? "Your parents? Both of them?"

Her eyes filled with stark pain. "Apparently my dad figured out what happened to my mother. How she'd disappeared. Somehow he found Petru, and joined Haru-Re as one of his followers, to be with her."

Shahin was getting a bad feeling about where this was going. "Gillian has actually seen your parents? Talked with them?

Gemma Swallowed and nodded. "Yeah."

He finally reached out to draw her into his arms, forcing a calmness he didn't feel. "I'm so sorry, *kalila*. I know this must be difficult for you."

But her body was stiff, unresponsive, and he felt a slight tremor in her limbs. *God help him*. He braced for what was coming next.

"I have to go there, Shahin. To Petru," she said quietly.

He froze. So much for her being bound to him during the sharing of magic.

"No," he said vehemently. Unbidden, his element started to rumble underfoot.

"Yes, I do. With Josslyn," she went on as though she didn't know he was on the verge of losing it. "We must surrender ourselves up to Haru-Re, and join his followers."

"What?" He couldn't believe he was hearing this. More earth tremors shook the tent.

She looked up at him with doleful eyes. "Don't you see? It's the obvious solution to this whole impossible situation."

The only thing he saw was that she must not

really be in love with him if she was ready and willing to leave him without backward glance and go over to his mortal enemy. If she truly loved him, she could never even think to betray him in such a way.

Well, to hell with that!

And her, too.

He clenched his teeth. Hard. The ground below quaked violently.

"Haru-Re has no interest in you," he snapped, too hurt by her suggestion to think about his heated response. Her lips pressed together, and he suddenly got the absurd notion that he'd hurt her with the statement. But that wasn't possible.

She turned away, wincing at the books flying off shelves that vibrated with his anger. "I'm very aware I'm not the sister anyone wants," she said evenly. "Joss is the one he wants, the one he traded Nephtys for. She's the only bargaining chip Khepesh has. But I cant let her go alone to Petru to be a hostage."

He couldn't answer. Speechless. Was she *kidding?*

"You want your priestess back, don't you? Besides, I belong with my family," she concluded. "And they're at Petru."

He finally found his tongue. "That's it?" He growled. The earth boomed and shook. "What about *us?*"

"*What* us?" she volleyed back at him, unafraid of falling objects or his fury. "You've made it pretty damn clear there *is* no us, and that you have no interest in making one!" Her shoulders straightened. "I'd be doing you a favour, leaving before you get *bored* with me."

Hot shame sliced through his chest hearing his own heartless words flung back at him.

Which melted his icy rage. And calmed the tremors thundering through the tent.

Okay. He deserved the rebuke. And had earned her blame. He'd been a total ass to say that. Even back then, he'd known it wasn't true. He'd just been in flat-out denial.

As he'd been up until this very minute.

"Gemma," he said, reining in the impulse to grab her and show her how *not* bored he was. How not bored he'd always be with her. How much he wanted her. For the long-term, not just a few days.

But he had to convince her calmly and logically. Not like a caveman.

A final shudder rocked the ground beneath them, then all went still and silent in the tent.

He took a deep breath. "You said you love me," he said, striving hard for cool reason and a calm demeanor.

Her shoulders slumped a tiny bit. "I *do* love you,"

she said, reluctance ringing in her voice. Misery shone in her beautiful eyes.

Hoped swelled his heart that this insane idea wasn't something she truly wanted. "Then...why?"

She sighed. "You once said the blood addiction works both ways, Shahin. Well, so does love. It has to, or it doesn't work at all."

He knew that. Better than most men.

His throat closed convulsively as fear welled up within him. He knew what must come next. It was his turn for confession. Time to make it right.

In all his years as a warrior, he'd never been this afraid. He was so afraid of committing himself to her. Afraid she would betray him in the end.

But most of all, he was afraid of losing her.

He couldn't lose her. He *couldn't*. And because of that, he was willing to take a chance on all the rest. He *must* take the chance.

He sucked down the fear and walked over to Gemma. He put his hands over the curve of those stiff, unyielding shoulders.

"But I *do* love you," he said.

For a moment she stood absolutely still. Then she slowly turned and looked up at him. Her eyes brimmed with wary caution. And something else....

Hopefulness?

"What did you say?" she asked, so softly he barely heard her words.

He slid his hands up and cupped her jaw. "I said I love you. I love you, Gemma Haliday, and I want you to stay with me here at Khepesh. For always."

He didn't add that if she ever tried to escape to Petru he'd hunt her down and tie her to his bed until he changed her mind, using any method at his disposal.

That would probably not be considered calm or reasonable.

Her tongue peeked out and slid over her lower lip. "Seriously?"

"I couldn't be more serious," he assured her, watching her tongue worry her lips. He finally gave in and covered her mouth with his. He kissed her until she surrendered, her body melting into his with deep sighs. "Believe me now?" he asked when their lips finally parted.

"Oh, yes," she whispered.

"And you'll stay with me?"

She smiled. "Oh, yes."

"No more talk of giving yourself to Haru-Re? Or to any other man?"

She shook her head. "Never. You're the only man I want, Shahin. The only man I've ever wanted."

That was more like it.

"Good," he said, and nodded. "So then you'll bind yourself to me. As my wife and consort."

She blinked. Hesitated. "Was that a question?"

"No," he said, and her brow wrinkled. "It was a proposal," he clarified.

Her brow smoothed. She smiled again. A brilliant, joyful smile. "In that case, yes," she answered. "Yes, I'll bind myself to you, Sheikh Shahin Aswadi, for as long as I live."

He kissed her again. And breathed a sigh of relief. Because he knew in his heart that this incredible, frustrating, courageous and spirited woman would love him well, and loyally, through all the remaining years of his life.

Nephtys had been so right.

This woman was his soul mate. Gemma was his destiny.

Epilogue

For the hundredth time that hour, Gemma gazed down at the gorgeous engagement ring on her finger. It was so beautiful she could hardly believe it was real.

But it was. When Shahin had offered to conjure one for her right after his proposal, she'd insisted on waiting for the real thing.

"I don't want it suddenly disappearing," she'd said with a grin.

That had been two days ago. She was still deliriously happy. She loved Shahin with all her heart, and he loved her. Once he'd confessed his love, he'd literally showered her with gifts and affection. The man was spoiling her, and she was basking in it.

Who'd have thought the notorious death warrior could have such sweet, tender feelings? She'd better not let it get out. His legendary bad-boy image would be all shot to hell.

The only thing marring their happiness was Seth. The demigod brooded day and night about the fate of his beloved sister, Nephtys, and true to his threat, he also refused to listen to a single word about Josslyn. She was still out there somewhere on her own, blissfully unaware she had been used as a pawn in a high-stakes game of supernatural palace intrigue.

But the vampire was in dire need of a blood sacrifice. He was growing weaker by the hour, and the *shemsu* of Khepesh were all beginning to worry. He had turned away any immortal woman who had offered him blood and had refused permission to seek a mortal aboveground who might accommodate his need. Gemma's sacrifice had not lasted long. He must have taken very little, indeed.

Shahin had even suggested to her that they offer to share magic again, just to get his friend to feed. Seeing how quickly Seth-Aziz was declining, she'd reluctantly agreed. But the vampire would have no part of it.

She was concerned for Seth. And she was even more concerned for Josslyn's safety. Something had to be done.

"Let it alone," Shahin had advised her as they lay in bed together that morning after making love, and she'd brought it up again. "Seth will come around soon. He has to."

But Gemma wasn't willing to take the chance with her sister's life. Shahin's spies had reported trouble brewing in Petru. The priestess Nephtys had refused to become Haru-Re's consort until she had performed some ritual which would take an entire year to complete, and the high priest of Re-Horakhti was beyond furious. Gemma was deathly afraid he would renege on his agreement to leave Joss alone. And angry as he was, she feared even more that the result would not be pretty.

She'd thought about it all day.

And decided there was only one thing left to do.

She stole quietly to the secret place where she'd hidden the small scroll that Gillian had given her in the dream, and gingerly pulled it out.

If the high priest Seth-Aziz wouldn't allow

Gemma to go out and bring her sister safely back to the palace…well, she really had no choice, did she?

Slowly she smiled and glanced at the scroll. She'd just have to get her sister to come to Khepesh all on her own….

* * * * *

HARLEQUIN®

nocturne™

COMING NEXT MONTH

Available November 30, 2010

#101 THE WOLVEN
The Keepers
Deborah LeBlanc

#102 ALASKAN WOLF
Alpha Force
Linda O. Johnston

HARLEQUIN®

A Romance

FOR EVERY MOOD™

Spotlight on

Classic

Quintessential, modern love stories
that are romance at its finest.

See the next page
to enjoy a sneak peek from
the Harlequin® Romance series.

*See below for a sneak peek from our classic
Harlequin® Romance® line.*

Introducing DADDY BY CHRISTMAS by Patricia Thayer.

M<small>IA</small> caught sight of Jarrett when he walked into the open lobby. It was hard not to notice the man. In a charcoal business suit with a crisp white shirt and striped tie covered by a dark trench coat, he looked more Wall Street than small-town Colorado.

Mia couldn't blame him for keeping his distance. He was probably tired of taking care of her.

Besides, why would a man like Jarrett McKane be interested in her? Why would he want to take on a woman expecting a baby? Yet he'd done so many things for her. He'd been there when she'd needed him most. How could she not care about a man like that?

Heart pounding in her ears, she walked up behind him. Jarrett turned to face her. "Did you get enough sleep last night?"

"Yes, thanks to you," she said, wondering if he'd thought about their kiss. Her gaze went to his mouth, then she quickly glanced away. "And thank you for not bringing up my meltdown."

Jarrett couldn't stop looking at Mia. Blue was definitely her color, bringing out the richness of her eyes.

"What meltdown?" he said, trying hard to focus on what she was saying. "You were just exhausted from lack of sleep and worried about your baby."

He couldn't help remembering how, during the night, he'd kept going in to watch her sleep. How strange was that? "I hope you got enough rest."

She nodded. "Plenty. And you're a good neighbor for

coming to my rescue."

He tensed. Neighbor? *What neighbor kisses you like I did?* "That's me, just the full-service landlord," he said, trying to keep the sarcasm out of his voice. He started to leave, but she put her hand on his arm.

"Jarrett, what I meant was you went beyond helping me." Her eyes searched his face. "I've asked far too much of you."

"Did you hear me complain?"

She shook her head. "You should. I feel like I've taken advantage."

"Like I said, I haven't minded."

"And I'm grateful for everything…"

Grasping her hand on his arm, Jarrett leaned forward. The memory of last night's kiss had him aching for another. "I didn't do it for your gratitude, Mia."

Gorgeous tycoon Jarrett McKane has never believed in Christmas—but he can't help being drawn to soon-to-be-mom Mia Saunders! Christmases past were spent alone…and now Jarrett may just have a fairy-tale ending for all his Christmases future!

Available December 2010, only from Harlequin® Romance®.

REQUEST YOUR FREE BOOKS!

2 FREE NOVELS PLUS 2 FREE GIFTS!

◆ HARLEQUIN®

nocturne™

Dramatic and Sensual Tales of Paranormal Romance.

YES! Please send me 2 FREE Harlequin® Nocturne™ novels and my 2 FREE gifts (gifts are worth about $10). After receiving them, if I don't wish to receive any more books, I can return the shipping statement marked "cancel." If I don't cancel, I will receive 4 brand-new novels every other month and be billed just $4.47 per book in the U.S. or $4.99 per book in Canada. That's a saving of at least 15% off the cover price! It's quite a bargain! Shipping and handling is just 50¢ per book.* I understand that accepting the 2 free books and gifts places me under no obligation to buy anything. I can always return a shipment and cancel at any time. Even if I never buy another book from Harlequin, the two free books and gifts are mine to keep forever.

238/338 HDN E9M2

Name _____ (PLEASE PRINT)

Address _____ Apt. #

City _____ State/Prov. _____ Zip/Postal Code

Signature (if under 18, a parent or guardian must sign)

Mail to the Reader Service:
IN U.S.A.: P.O. Box 1867, Buffalo, NY 14240-1867
IN CANADA: P.O. Box 609, Fort Erie, Ontario L2A 5X3

Not valid for current subscribers to Harlequin Nocturne books.

Want to try two free books from another line?
Call 1-800-873-8635 or visit www.ReaderService.com.

* Terms and prices subject to change without notice. Prices do not include applicable taxes. N.Y. residents add applicable sales tax. Canadian residents will be charged applicable provincial taxes and GST. Offer not valid in Quebec. This offer is limited to one order per household. All orders subject to approval. Credit or debit balances in a customer's account(s) may be offset by any other outstanding balance owed by or to the customer. Please allow 4 to 6 weeks for delivery. Offer available while quantities last.

Your Privacy: Harlequin Books is committed to protecting your privacy. Our Privacy Policy is available online at www.ReaderService.com or upon request from the Reader Service. From time to time we make our lists of customers available to reputable third parties who may have a product or service of interest to you. If you would prefer we not share your name and address, please check here. ☐

Help us get it right—We strive for accurate, respectful and relevant communications. To clarify or modify your communication preferences, visit us at www.ReaderService.com/consumerschoice.

HN10

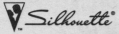

Sparked by Danger, Fueled by Passion.

RACHEL LEE
A Soldier's Redemption

When the Witness Protection Program fails at keeping Cory Farland out of harm's way, ex-marine Wade Kendrick steps in. As Cory's new bodyguard, Wade has a plan for protecting her—however falling in love was not part of his plan.

*Available in December
wherever books are sold.*

Visit Silhouette Books at www.eHarlequin.com

SRS27705

Silhouette® Desire

USA TODAY bestselling authors

MAUREEN CHILD

and

SANDRA HYATT

UNDER THE MILLIONAIRE'S MISTLETOE

Just when these leading men thought they had it all figured out, they quickly learn their hearts have made other plans. Two passionate stories about love, longing and the infinite possibilities of kissing under the mistletoe.

Available December wherever you buy books.

Always Powerful, Passionate and Provocative.

SD73069